THE
MOUNTAIN
CROWN

THE MOUNTAIN CROWN

KARIN LOWACHEE

SOLARIS

First published 2024 by Solaris
an imprint of Rebellion Publishing Ltd,
Riverside House, Osney Mead,
Oxford, OX2 0ES, UK

www.solarisbooks.com

ISBN: 978-1-83786-239-9

10 9 8 7 6 5 4 3 2 1

A CIP catalogue record for this book is available from the
British Library.

Designed & typeset by Rebellion Publishing

Printed in Denmark

EVEN THE AIR around Fortune City tasted dirty. Méka felt it like a mucus of smoke and waste on the flat of her tongue. She spat on the deck of the river barge. The Mountain Guard who'd climbed aboard to check the papers of the passengers watched her do it, his lips curling with a familiar disdain. She'd witnessed the same expression on the crew of the whaling ship that had brought her north to this island that was once her home. As if she no longer belonged in the land of her ancestors.

She didn't look away from the Guard and he approached with the stiff-legged swagger of a typical Kattakan. His energetic presence was a hollow clang to her, an empty bucket struck by the hammer of the cosmos. The infestation of Kattakans to Ba'Suon land created ceaseless echoes of nothingness. Even the wind carried a fervor of life these Kattakans lacked. She had not felt such absence among so much living nature in ten years. Despite her parents' warning before she embarked on this journey, the absence was nearly impossible to tolerate, as was the condescension and arrogance from people like this Mountain Guard.

His sun-lined eyes roved from her shorn hair to the gray dappled suon scales stitched into the wool and fox-fur collar of her coat. His gaze lingered on the rifle slung on her shoulder. "You plan to use that, Bastard?"

"No." Her people were not prone to violence but this was not a language Kattakans understood.

He grunted and continued his staring assessment of her attire. She was the only Ba'Suon aboard the barge; all the other passengers were the same ilk of desperate homeless hoping for a better opportunity in the gold fields or in town. The clog of boats along the river, both steam and paddle of every size and craftsmanship, seemed unceasing in its traffic. So many foolish individuals hoping to strike it rich, or exploit one another, or perhaps with little inclination to find another path. She was now a part of the throng, not for the gold but for the suon, though perhaps no less foolish for the journey no matter how necessary the rite.

The Guard waved his hand at the chains crisscrossed over her chest. "What're those for?"

"I could show you but I'd need to call one of those suon closer."

Four of the creatures circled overhead in muted ellipses, dull shadows against the canvas sack color of the sky. *Dragons*, the Kattakans called them, but they were suon: creatures of fire to the Ba'Suon. Perhaps these suon were wild but their proximity to Fortune City and the subdued waves around them told Méka they were probably enslaved to the gold like the indentured people digging below. They were no threat, they barely disturbed her senses for how tethered they were to the work of these Kattakans, but the Guard glanced upward quickly as though one of them could breathe flames onto his head at any moment. He caught her watching his reaction and flicked a hand at the black twin blades hitched to her belt. "And those?"

She stated the obvious. "I'm Ba'Suon. These are Ba'Suon blades. If there is some sort of law against them, you're welcome to try and take them from me."

He was armed, a pistol in a holster on his belt, his navy woolen jacket a ragged testimony to the weather he endured here during harsher months. He squinted into her eyes as if he expected her to look away. She didn't. This was not a Kattakan used to taking the initiative. He seemed to come to a temperate conclusion and held out his hand. "Papers."

She delivered them from the pouch at the front of her coat. He read through both sheets, front and back, staring a heartbeat longer at the stamps issued by his Kattakan government and the attached card from the government of the southern isle from which she'd traveled. Both supposedly gave her permission to cross the border, but she had known coming here for the first time since the end of the war that there was no telling what agreements would stand. She had volunteered for the seasonal rite to allow her this access rather than her parents or anyone else in the family Suonkang. It was time she saw their land with her adult eyes, instead of with the emotional vision of the dream that plagued her. A dream like this was a message from the cosmos and she had no choice but to follow its path in order to glean the meaning.

"Where're you coming from?" said the Guard, even as he read her papers.

"That is the stamp of Mazemoor."

"And why're you here?"

He held her permit in his hand but she answered anyway. "To gather suon."

"You know you can't use your Bastard magic in Kattaka around our people."

"I'm aware."

"Where you aim to get 'em?"

She looked pointedly toward the Crown Mountains looming in jagged majesty beyond the hills and plateaus around Fortune City.

"How you gonna get there?"

"The most expedient course would be to hire a horse."

"You ain't allowed to fly those dragons back."

It was an entire other protocol to register a gathered suon and he must have known that. Just like he knew the answers to everything else he asked her. So she didn't bother to answer him again.

They were paranoid about the wild suon, with reason. On the borders of Fortune City stood wooden tower emplacements for iron cannons aimed to the sky.

His gaze flitted toward them then looked all around the deck of the barge, the crates wrapped in rope and oiled canvas and the two dozen other passengers milling about. Another Mountain Guard moved among them asking for identification. He looked back at Méka.

"Rifle."

She unslung it from her shoulder and handed it over because pointing out the waste of time would only delay her further. He folded her papers and pocketed them, then seized the rifle in both of his hands at stock and forestock. With perfunctory movements he braced the butt of the weapon to his shoulder and sighted down the barrel. Then he angled it down and slid back the bolt. The rifle was unloaded. He seemed disappointed, as if she should have been breaking the law by carrying it live to the town. He locked it and passed the weapon back to her. She slung it back on her shoulder. He retrieved her papers from his pocket, looked at them and looked at her, then he held them out as if she were somehow forcing him in this dance. With a twist of her lips she accepted them and he moved past her to the next passenger.

She hauled up from her feet the lumpen bag of her supplies and draped it over her other shoulder. Another gust of gritty air brushed against her cheek, carrying the scent of mud and unwashed bodies. For Kattakans, gold as both idea and allure alone defined the ambitiously named Fortune City, where nearly ten thousand dream-laden people pitted the wilderness bank like debris left behind by an army long decamped. Méka had come to this river mouth with her family in her childhood, when the terrain had been untouched, but she barely remembered it. She had been perhaps five years old the last time. Soon after, she and many other Ba'Suon families were corralled into camps by the Kattakans who had settled this island by force.

It was early summer and steam rose up off the wet land at the mouth of the Derish River. A delicate mist breathed over all of the angled tents and crooked cabins hewn from green lumber. The flat façades of public emporiums were lined up along Shore Street, with their weathered, upswept lettering mimicking the décor of a civilization hundreds of miles away. It was a ghost town, not for a lack of population but for the empty carousing that gripped these souls hanging on to some semblance of a life remembered. Méka couldn't understand such a life. Her family had quit this land and its overseers after the war ten years ago so they didn't have to witness it. But the sky and the cosmos bore witness as they had since creation and rang with a stifled fury, the reverberations of which she felt in her Ba'Suon blood. If her dream foretold some sort of reckoning for the imbalance, perhaps this journey would enlighten her to it.

Overhead, the shades of low-flying suon still spun, indistinguishable from the sadness of bondage to this town. This far north the summer night sank to twilight blue, when the suon yearned for pitch night and nests. These suon got neither. She wanted to call them to her to soothe, but any outstretch toward them was met with fear and she watched as they darted higher, further away from the river. A faint whistling of air fluted through their hollow scales as they sailed updrafts with the mountains as backdrop. Once these ranges had been free for both suon and the Ba'Suon. Her parents and their parents stretching back as far as families remembered had grown with the mountains and its life. Now only the highest peaks stood liberated from the greed and scrabble below, for no other reason than because the Kattakans' need for gold could not tame them.

HER BOOTS SANK into the sandbar up to her ankles as she made her way inland toward Shore Street. A bazaar of people hawked various wares from their decimated outfits—shovels, pots and pans, long johns, even bread for the wealthy. The smell was irrepressible: unwashed bodies and sawdust, piss and dogs and exhausted horseflesh that quivered untied by a log pile, forgotten. The animal's presence passed through her like a fog.

She kept walking. The constant grind of the sawmills buzzed insistent against her ears, masking all of nature. Shore Street wasn't much of a street, as most of the ground was mud so thick even the mules battled to take a step. Duckboards sagged in the soup of it, weighted by the constant shuffle of bodies milling before shops, gambling dens, dance halls and saloons, open at all hours. Sullen faces looked at her but didn't see her. The nothingness of these Kattakans tried to stick to her like oil. She breathed shallow so as not to imbibe their lives.

She interrupted a line stretching across her path for fifty feet. The head of it disappeared somewhere in a small post office. People stood with barely enough space between them and every few minutes they inched forward as toward a lectern of judgment, their heads down, their hands pocketed. On the other side of the queue a crowd spilled in a disorderly glut from twin doors held open by sheer numbers. Gusts of smoke expelled above their heads. From within, the bulbous sounds of indistinct voices swelled and burst in response to some action unseen from the street.

i in the blood i and you

She startled and looked up. Unlike the other buildings in the row, this wooden structure arched in a blackened dome above the roofs of its neighbors. Smoke billowed from narrow slats between beams. A rough-hewn sign hung above the doors with the words emblazoned: *Pit Dragon Emporium.*

i and the claw and you
blood and the tooth and blood in eyes

The wrongness of it jarred her, like a finger shoving between her ribs, through her skin and muscle. All of the town receded like an ocean sucked back into the gluttonous firmament of the clouds. She tasted cinder in her mouth, inside her nose.

She shouldered her way through the clog. Once inside, the glaucoma-white of daylight dimmed to near blindness. Incense smoke mingled with a sharper scent, something from the boil of the earth itself. The stink of suon fear, imprisoned by the press bodies.

torn wing and choke i
scream in burst i blood and you

Her throat seized and she coughed to open it again. Between the long arms of diggers come in from the gold trenches and tattered ex-soldiers with their uniform badges smeared by dirt, a woman sat behind an overturned crate. On the top lay strips of dark salted meat. The woman hollered through the bodies, offering dragon cuts for a finger of coin. Méka swung away, swallowing rage with suon rage pulsing toward her.

i in blood and you and i
shadow and cry

She shoved deeper into the crowd. Hollow masks made of wood and shale hung from poles screwed into the tall walls. They resembled a child's version of a suon face, haphazardly painted around the eyes with red and white. The onlookers separated slightly when she pushed closer to an iron cage erected in the center of the space, a skeleton in the domed shape of the emporium itself. Inside the cage two suon fought, tethered to chains that anchored their long necks.

i and blood and i

She could not discern from which suon came the impression. A blast of unseen waves crashed against her and she flailed. She failed to touch either of them, all of her awareness ricocheting back to her in panicked rebuff. The disturbance to nature nearly rocked her on her feet.

A piebald cloud and a black suon. They were adolescent in size, twice the height of a tall man when reared on their hindquarters. Their leathery wings were bound to their bodies by winch rope. Long jaws snapped at each other in ducking feint and leaping attack. Their golden eyes rolled and darted. Legs and flanks and whipping tails jarred the cage in the violence of the bout and the crowd erupted in sounds of fear and excitement, the tumult echoing up to the rafters. Hands reached above the sea of heads, exchanging bills and bets. On the edges of the cage bars, blood slicked the iron like sweat, reflecting a dull crimson gleam.

i in the blood and you and tooth
goldshard

She looked toward the bursting impression of sunlight, incongruous in this pit. Near the iron plate bolted to the floorboards, with the chain slithering and rattling as the cloud suon strained and jerked, a man with a wide-brimmed hat pulled low over his eyes crouched and rocked on the pads of his feet. He was barefoot, skin blackened by soot. He paid no mind to anything but the fight. The ebony suon struck the cloud suon with a fore-talon and the cloud shrieked and stumbled. A barrage of incoherent pain pummeled against her and Méka clamped around her own reaction, didn't bristle, a subtle attempt to soothe. Sweat trickled down the back of her neck and nausea rose in her throat. The cloud suon's chain cracked against wood and iron.

The *goldshard* man flinched and made a hissing sound between his teeth as if he felt the suon's pain like she felt it, though no Kattakan should. No Kattakan should have ever felt so acutely of *goldshard*. They were hollow, soundless. A gouging instrument to all of nature.

An image from her dream blared unbidden before her eyes: a yellow field of grass and an incandescent sun, making the entire world shimmer in its light. A man in the distance, his back to her, a halo of blood red around his shoulders. This man?

i and blood i and gold

i shiver and i

The shadows and noise of the pit swelled up around her once more, a pulsing echo from the piebald suon, blood from its heart pumping its distress through the arteries of the earth. She stared as this man reached toward it, but instead of a left hand he lightly tapped the iron bars with a leather-wrapped stump. The suon's eyes rolled toward him, breath panting in hot gusts. It hunkered down near to his position on the other side of the cage, an unsteady rumble from the bottom of its throat like rockfall in an avalanche. He stroked the long neck with the edge of his handless wrist.

Onlookers closest around the cage began to bang on it with tin cups and broken shovel handles. Two men standing on the opposite side took hold of the chain that bound the black suon and heaved to pull it back from the cloud, which had fallen to its side and blew labored air like a bellows. More gashes showed along its skinned ribs where scales should have been. The black roared, muzzle peeled back, its molten dark tongue fluttering in the heated air. Tendrils of smoke eked from flared nostrils. It had only one fang.

Méka turned and elbowed her way out. The screams of the suon pierced her eardrums still and racketed in her mind like a gale. The edges of her sight dimmed even standing once more under the cold white sky. She tried to breathe clean but everywhere smelled of Kattakan stink and despair.

A mélange of sensations and images melted behind her eyes, crawled over her skin. *gold and í* lingered like a corona around the edges of it all. That man. His shared energy with the suon. The impossibility of him like reaching up and feeling the burn of the stars. She moved before she realized she was moving, battling the conflicting urges to return to the emporium and run away from it before she immolated.

She trudged through the oily mud until she found herself in a saloon and leaned at the bar for a rice beer. The same here as in Mazemoor, as in all towns of a certain size. The murky familiarity of the scene grounded her with some steadiness. She balanced against the seating. Here she could focus on simple realities. Watery alcohol but she drank it anyway. In the corner a white-haired fellow plied piano keys, half of which were missing. He rocked to the side and smiled at her, his grin as gap-toothed as the instrument. The room pressed in on her, barely fifteen feet at its widest point, the walls smoke-stained, the floorboards dredged with dirt, sawdust, and eggshells. Voices caroled behind her with oblivious revelry and she blinked slowly down at the foggy amber of her drink, finding some false fortune in its depths.

She was so absorbed in the narrow focus of the glass that she didn't feel a thing until another woman leaned beside her and asked the bartender for a shot. Then she spoke to Méka in a dialect of the western families of the Ba'Suon. The sound of her in Méka's mind was a slow susurration, faint but present, like distant waves. A strange relief. She asked Méka if she had just arrived in Fortune City.

"Came straight to the saloon." A lie so she needn't describe the pit dragon emporium. One required a drink to deal with Kattakans, with what she'd just witnessed. She looked at the woman and recognized the visage of her people in the dark eyes and saturnine expression. Harsh lines scored the woman's cheeks and slashed across her forehead like a washing cloth wrung of all moisture. Her hair hung long and stringy, not shaved and clean, and she wore the clothing of a Kattakan miner: corduroy shoulders and the straight plain edges of labor denim. At her waist sat a single blade, not the twin of their people. Perhaps the blade wasn't even her own and this woman had never completed a rite of gathering. For all Méka knew this Ba'Suon in Kattakan garb had stolen it in dishonor.

The thought coiled snake-like in Méka's belly. "You work in the valley."

The woman tossed back her shot. "The Gold Kings require dragons and the dragons require Bastards to be their 'dragoneers.'"

So she was someone who spoke to the suon that winged above the town, the ones who fled in fear at the touch of a Ba'Suon. Small wonder if this woman was the extent of their acquaintance.

"You call them your kings?" Méka said. "And dragons?"

She got a dismissive wave in reply. "I see your suon scales and you think because you left your home paths that you can come back to mine and judge me?"

The woman was already half-drunk. Who knew how long she'd been sitting in this saloon. Méka turned away and motioned to the barkeep to top up her glass. "Whatever you desire, sister."

"Working with the suon keeps them out of the pit."

She drank, eyes on the backbar. "Not all of them."

"They were in the war. There's nothing for them but the pit, they are battle caught."

She looked at the woman again. So this was what they told themselves, the Ba'Suon who served the gold towns. "Were you in the war?"

The woman grunted and hunched over her shot glass as if to protect it. The hum of their connection prickled now like static electricity. "You're too young to remember."

"My family was in the camps. For ten years."

"Then you were fortunate. Though I hear it's worse living in Mazemoor with their dirty magic."

"No worse than here and the absence of it."

The woman didn't answer or look at her. She picked up her glass and wandered off as if some remote voice called to her.

Méka turned and peered at the mirror of the backbar, seeing it all at once. It was chipped black in places with a couple bullet holes and cobwebs of cracks spidering outward. Some of the murky green and brown glass bottles were layered in thin films of dust. On the shelf a tiny rocking horse made of black soapstone. Antler bone the length of her arm. When she looked again into the mirror a shadow in the shape of a man stood directly behind her, but the longer she watched the more indistinct he became. She turned around but saw nothing, only the carousing Kattakans and that Ba'Suon woman at a corner table staring at her. The door to the saloon swung as if some sudden wind from inside had gusted it open. She looked back at the Ba'Suon woman. In the duration of moments between her sighting the shadow in the mirror and the movement at the door, all sound had disappeared as though suctioned out of the world by a massive explosion.

"Did you see who that was?" she asked the Ba'Suon. Her own voice sounded tinny despite her pitching it to bridge the distance between them, to be heard above the ringing piano.

"Be grateful you didn't," said the woman, looking down at her drink, shoulders bowed.

A cold sank through Méka's skin and settled in her chest. "What do you mean by that?"

But the other Ba'Suon woman didn't answer.

WHEN MÉKA EMERGED from the saloon the sky above had deepened to stone blue and faded to a burnt and angry orange behind the western mountain peaks, casting them in silhouette like an illuminated shadow box. The city sounded louder and cavernous in the northern night. All the chatter, laughter, and music spilled directionless from various saloons and parlors up and down the muddy thoroughfare. Deep between buildings where alleyways forged bitter shadows, summer dropped hard with the sinking of the sun.

She thought of hiring a horse to quit this town at the fastest possible speed but a silence from the direction of the pit dome told her the fights had ended. She couldn't feel the suon and could not walk on from them. Exposed once again to the sky, the remembrance of the piebald's screams came to her in phantom echoes.

She walked behind the venue. Its doors were shut now with a sign swung around to tell of the next bout in the morning. She found the stables where the suon were kept. Idling outside of it was the man with the stump.

goldshard í and í

The soft sleeping whisper of the suon emanated from inside the stables. In the relative quiet of the man's presence she felt *bloodred* mingled in it like a stain. A strange combination if it weren't already disturbing to get any impression of him at all. Her dream refracted at the back of her mind like looking at an image through leaded glass. But there was no sun, only shadows.

He sat on an upended wooden pail. He'd found a pair of rubber boots and with his single hand he held a cigarette burning between his knees. Above his head a beaten metal lantern hung from the door of the stables, yellow and blurred, barely offering light. She couldn't see his eyes beneath his hat. He had a short russet beard grown in the manner of most Kattakan men, but he didn't feel like most Kattakan men.

He noticed her. "They're asleep." He took a drag from the cigarette. The cherry burned like a microcosm of his own energy smeared across her awareness. "You're Ba'Suon."

"It's so."

"You come for the dragons?"

"Are you their keeper?"

"Na. I'm as kept as they are." He shook a leg and only then did she see the iron shackle around his right ankle and the chain of it bolted to the wall of the stables.

She tried to feel any anger from him, the way any Kattakan could expend anger so blunt it could be discerned without Ba'Suon knowing, but there was none. Only a kind of resignation. The despair from this city sank a little more into her bones. "Who's your keeper?"

The man waved his leatherbound stump vaguely toward the rest of the town.

"What's their name?"

"Why?"

She set her sack on the ground and shifted the rifle on her shoulder. The man tilted back his chin and regarded her with the faint glimmer of blue eyes. Those eyes marked the two blades at her side. He was not as old as she'd first thought, perhaps her brother's age. A little older than her.

"You know suon," she said.

He shrugged.

"How did you learn the suon?"

He took another pull from the cigarette. "A fellar in the war, in my unit. He was Ba'Suon like you."

Some of her people had served rather than rotting in Kattakan camps like her family. None of those volunteers had returned to their ancestral paths after the war. Like the woman in the saloon, they were mired here in employ to wealthy Kattakans who sought Ba'Suon skills but despised the practitioners.

She said, "What was his name?"

"Sephihalé ele Janan."

Kattakans always said Ba'Suon names backwards. This man did not.

"I know the family Sephihalé. Their path crossed the Derish every summer." Like her family's had, and down across the lesser rivers where now Kattakans sifted for gold.

"And now they're all scattered to the wind," he said.

A flash of *goldshard* flickered at her, then dimmed just as quickly, and she realized what she felt from this man was something of the family Sephihalé. As if he'd lived long enough among them to be seen by the stars.

"What's your name?" she said.

He flicked the butt of his cigarette toward her. It landed a foot away and snuffed in the mud. He looked into the shadows and his presence seemed to diffuse as if in search of the gloom.

"Why are you shackled?"

"I owed a debt."

A heavy blackness moved on her right. A thick-set Kattakan woman in tall rubber boots and a longcoat materialized from the dark between the pit dome and the stables.

The woman stopped. "Who are you?"

This tone of voice like the Mountain Guard. Méka set her hand on the hilt of one of her blades. "I come to ask after this man and the piebald cloud."

"Ask what?"

"How much to buy them out?"

She felt the man look at her. He moved as if to rise, but stopped when the woman looked his way.

"Are you joking?" the woman said.

"How much?" Méka said.

"Get out of here, Bastard."

Méka lifted her sack and dug into it. Then she tossed a leather bag the size of her hand toward the woman. It landed on the ground and the contents rang loud.

"What the fuck is this?"

Méka said, "Three gold bars. You can weigh them."

The woman grabbed up the bag and searched inside. Lifted out one of the narrow bars and held it toward the wan lantern light, then up toward the sky as if seeking verification from the moon. "Bastard gold," she said.

"More pure than what you'll find down at the creeks."

The woman set the end of the bar between her teeth and gnawed. She looked at it again, then looked at Méka. "What you want this stumpy soldier for?"

"Is it a deal?"

The woman wormed her fingers into her coat pocket and tossed an iron key at the man's feet. "The dragon's your responsibility. Creature's no use after that last bout anyway."

It was unclear whether she was speaking to Méka or to the man.

MÉKA AND THE man stood alone outside the stable doors. The shackle and chain sat in an empty haphazard coil in the mud. Standing, he was barely level with her height and slouched slightly under some unseen weight.

"Why did you do that?" he said.

"You're free to go," she told him, "but if you're interested in work, I can pay you."

"What kinda work?"

"I need a hand with the cloud for the next few weeks."

"Doin what?"

"I'm going to the mountains to gather."

"Gather dragons?"

She nodded once.

"You got a permit for that?"

"Yes."

"You gonna gather them dragons on Crown Mountain all by yourself?"

"Just one dragon. Maybe two with your help."

"King dragons, right. To stud."

So he was familiar with the rite. She nodded again.

He half-laughed. "You Ba'Suon are insane."

"You know what'll happen if there're too many kings nested with the wild crowns."

She saw in his eyes that he did. Yet he asked, as if to test her: "What?"

"We heard all the way on the south isle that Fortune City had burned down once before."

He measured her for a moment. Then he looked toward the pit dome. "You think them wild dragons know?"

"Know what?"

"What we do here."

"Close enough and they likely feel it." As she felt it. The heavy sadness.

The man looked at the stable doors behind which slept the suon. "Then what? If you get your kings."

"Then I'll take them south to my people in Mazemoor."

"All the way to another fuckin island?"

"Do you want the work or not?"

"I guess I'll take it. But I only got one hand."

"I noticed. Open the stables."

He didn't move like he lacked a hand. He fished out another key from his shirt pocket, opened the padlock with deft fingers and swung back both doors one after the other. "Name's Lilley."

She moved past him into the small dim interior. It smelled like suon waste, a sharp chemical scent, and old wood and burnt embers. "Suonkang ele Mékahalé."

He said behind her. "Mékahalé."

"Méka's fine."

Two of the four stalls stood empty. She strode between them and passed the black suon first. Tendrils of its presence reached toward her like smoke.

i and hunger and cloud

It huffed in restless sleep, nose to tail, shackled as Lilley had been. Its inky scales shone dully from what little moonlight and midnight sky eked through the window slats on the ceiling. Northern suon were primarily nocturnal, but forced into Kattakan labor they took their sleep when they could. She walked on. The far leftmost stall held the piebald cloud.

i and blood i sting and breathe i hurt

She sucked in a breath. Lilley followed and told her to stand back, the cloud knew him and wouldn't fuss. She watched from the stable bay as he stepped in the stall and unhooked the chain from the wall and coiled the loose end of it around his forearm stump. The chain led to a leather halter but he didn't unhook it. He hissed at the cloud suon and clicked his teeth and hissed again until its golden eyes opened and it lifted its chin confused. Méka saw from the round arch of its brow that it was a female.

i and shiver and cold i

"I call her Cottontooth." Lilley smiled and the piebald cloud bumped her muzzle against his shoulder. An impression of *goldcloud* wafted toward Méka, the suon's recognition of the man and herself. Méka breathed out, watching as the sharp edges of the creature seemed to soften in the Kattakan's presence.

Under the shadows it was impossible to tell the extent of her injuries from the pit but when she lumbered to her feet she seemed to favor her right haunch. Lilley continued to hiss and click at her as he guided her from the stall, waving his other arm at Méka to tell her to precede him. The suon tasted the air and tilted her head, sensing an unknown body. Coming awake, she still barely hummed in Méka's mind. Just slow low waves of *i in i blue night and you...*

Méka waited for them in the mud between pit dome and weathered stables. They were slow to emerge. Lilley coaxed the battered suon all the way, stroking her neck continuously. When she stepped free from the confines of her prison she flung back her head to taste the sky. The amber eyes rolled and nostrils flared, but she made no smoke. She must have expected a fight, drawn out of slumber only for battle.

i in night and blood and i cloudsky

Méka tested the edges of the suon's awareness but Cottontooth didn't look at her or respond to the impression of openness. "Free her wings," Méka said.

"She'll fly."

"Do it."

Méka moved close enough to touch the suon's neck, her palm flat along the shifting scales as the beast breathed in distressed huffs.

í ín níght ínsíde and blood and í ín tongue and cold ín í

The prospect of freedom frightened her. Méka could feel the thick pulse pounding and looked over at Lilley. He stood with a blade in his hand and shook his head.

cloudsky

"Now," Méka said.

He sliced through the winch ropes where they cinched around the softer underbelly. On instinct the suon flexed her wings and the loose ropes stretched. Then she fluttered her wings in fits and managed to cast off the cutting lines. She threw her head back and bellowed. Lilley winced from the sound and planted his feet, his arm taut and the chain shifting tight around it as he tried to anchor the suon when she arched her neck and extended her wings fully. The span of them blocked out the moon and rose beyond the roof of the stables, banners of bone-white with the vague blue night shining through the thinnest stretch of skin.

Méka called to her in the dialect of the Suonkang and stroked her along the neck. When Cottontooth ducked her chin, she rubbed beneath it and along the plate-hard muzzle and up between flared white brows.

cloudsky cloudstars cloudmoon

Freedom. Méka walked along her flank, running her hand across the bicolored scales of gray and white, avoiding the exposed flesh of old wounds and absent armor but feeling the girth and strength of her, the solid muscles of her hindquarters. Though she was missing lines of scales from her battles, the rest of her paneling felt secure. The calming hum in Méka's mind echoed back from the suon and it filled the canals of her ears like the roar of seashells.

She reached up and took hold of the halter. Cottontooth let her and Méka gestured for Lilley to unravel the chain from around his arm. In a few careful motions she freed the suon from the last piece of Kattakan shackles and let it fall to the mud. The long white head swung down, the angles and curves of which seemed carved from ivory. Within the deep eye sockets the avian-like gaze fixed on Méka.

i and sister and i

Méka looked back, tears forming a faint film over her vision. "Tei," she whispered. Go.

i and stars and stars and night and i

The humming bloomed to a roar in Méka's ears, then ceased as Cottontooth seized control of herself. The wings beat twice and the suon reared back on her hind legs, her taloned feet leaving deep imprints in the mud.

She launched herself into the air. The fury of it stirred the collar of Méka's coat. The scales stitched within the wool whispered as if in reply to the great whistling refrain of the suon's body. The wind of her flight pushed through her hard hollow scales until both suon and song disappeared into the night and the low dark clouds.

THE SILENCE AFTER sounded vast, the town ribaldry from the twisting streets just an echo fading into nothing. Lilley looked at her with shadows of confusion darkening his voice.

"Thought you needed that dragon?"

"She needed to be free first."

"She made a racket. They ain't gonna like it, we shoulda let her go outside the town. They might fire on her."

Méka heard no cannons, nor felt any rage from the suon. She looked at him closer. It wasn't fear in his tone, but weary caution. "How could you be in that pit with them and not free them?"

His shoulders straightened. "There ain't pits in Mazemoor?"

"No."

"I find that hard to believe."

"The suon remember," she said. "Through generations."

His jaw shifted like he tasted something bad. "I couldn't do nothin without bein shot myself."

The sooner they quit this place the better. She picked up her gear again. Lilley idled, looking at her as if for instruction, the silent stables behind him. A sudden caul of silence dampened all of nature around her, and the two of them for a moment of blinking were caught in the stasis of it.

She stood frozen, disoriented until from one breath to the next the world of this northern city burst with life again: the echoes of voices from nearby streets, the glow of streetlamps now haloed across the roofs of the buildings, the scent of neglected bodies and refuse dripping through the air. The moon extra bright in the bruised gray pallor of the sky.

Lilley's keeper returned to view from around the pit dome. She brought a man in a layered dark suit, wide hat and mustache, the beady glare of suspicion gleaming in his eyes. The air seemed to tighten around him, and with every contraction more of the world disappeared from Méka's senses. A pressure seemed to squeeze her ears until she dropped her hand to the hilt of one of her blades and with the force of her knowing, she shoved at the pressure until it burst.

The world rushed in again and this silent man shrouded in shadow stepped back as if he'd felt it physically. The echo of him had been in the saloon. She squinted to make out his shape now, but he seemed too indistinct in the night, his edges bleeding like ink across a cloth.

The woman was staring at Méka but spared a glance for the man retreating into the alley. She didn't call him back. "You gonna come with us now," she told them.

"Why?" Méka's grip tightened on the leather wrappings of the blade.

The woman removed her right hand from inside her jacket. She held a pistol.

"You come with us, Bastard," said the woman. "You too, Lilley."

"What's he doin here, Volla?" Lilley cast his gaze toward the alley. "One new Ba'Suon comes to town and he gotta get involved?"

The man emerged from the mouth of the alley once more but stepped no further. Méka tested a touch toward him but got nothing back, not even an echo like the other Kattakans. The silence did not balloon toward her but seemed shrunken tight around him like a funeral veil to keep out the sight of the living.

"Who are you?" Méka called to him.

"He's a traitor," Lilley said.

"Shut your mouths and come with us, we won't ask again," said the woman Volla.

Lilley put away his blade. Méka regarded the company, then slowly tightened the rope of her sack and threw it over the opposite shoulder from her unloaded rifle. She followed the Kattakans and heard Lilley trail behind her, his steps muted in the mud. The woman walked with the imperious air of one who held a secret or an advantage.

"Can I have a cigarette?" Lilley asked Volla.

"No."

They headed down Shore Street and passed dance halls where people loitered outdoors in sweaty deshabille. Others tottered toward saloon or hotel, or a dumpling house open every hour for the hungry who could pay. They walked to the far end of the street where stood a two-storey building with a wide porch and red awning, not a façade but the strong construction of an edifice made to withstand the northern wind and heavy weathering. The flat sign pasted above the awning read *Mountain Guard & Administration*.

She hadn't broken any laws that she knew of, but maybe that made no difference in this place. Maybe they were indeed displeased about her release of the piebald cloud, though she'd bought it out and had two witnesses to that fact. Inside, Volla pointed to a wooden bench against the wall and without a word Lilley went to it and sat. The silent, funereal man didn't look at any of them as he disappeared behind one of two doors leading to inner chambers.

Méka eyed the reception room, the relatively clean wooden floors, the two long banner scrolls reiterating that this was the office of the Mountain Guard. Black and white portraits hung on the walls, men and women in stiff-collared shirts with serious expressions on their frozen faces. They seemed to be thinking of indictments to place upon all who entered this building. Behind the desk on the wall was a large topographical map with small brass pins stuck in certain places all over the line-drawn terrain. She spied the Derish River label and around it the other names the Kattakans had given the land and its features, some of them bastardized from Ba'Suon dialects, some of them completely different—names in the Kattakan tongue.

"What is this about?" Méka said.

"You better siddown, missy," said Volla, parking herself at the corner of the desk.

Méka remained standing. Lilley gazed up at the ceiling with his head resting back on the wall as if to prop it straight. By and by, the inner door slid open again and a tall man entered. He wore a thick navy-blue tunic that for all its bulk seemed to adhere to his muscular form, and straight trousers lined on the outside edges with a dyed red leather strip. The cuffs were tucked into tall black boots immaculately clean, and his hair and beard fell long but neatly groomed, ash gray and black in stripes like a badger. A man who spoke and others listened to. Volla went to stand by the inner door. Lilley looked at the man without moving, just his eyes half-hidden beneath the low draw of his hat. The big Kattakan went to the desk and sat against it, motioning Méka to one of the chairs.

She stayed where she was and his iron eyes narrowed.

"I'm Lord Shearoji. I'm responsible for this city and its safety. You released a dragon without my authorization."

She looked at the other woman in the room. "It was a fair deal agreed upon by this person." She looked back at Shearoji. "And she took my gold."

"The gold was for the man. Dragon sales are under my purview."

"There's no law stating that."

"I'm stating it now."

"Is the pit fighting also under your purview?"

His stare didn't leave her face. "Yes it is. I take it you

don't approve, but that's not your call. We can't have untethered dragons flying around Fortune City."

But they could possess indentured Ba'Suon to control the suon, yet understood so little about that relationship. "The suon isn't untethered, she's just not tethered by iron and abuse."

"You have no guarantee of that."

"I'm a free Ba'Suon born of this land. I released her and your town isn't burning."

On the wall hung a clock, its hand ticking around a flame-carved circumference. They all heard it in the brief silence. Lord Shearoji's impatience whirlpooled about his shoulders, expanding toward her. Not a Ba'Suon impression, nor like the suon. But the force of his demand impossible to ignore, he was carved from it. This expectation of obedience.

"The town isn't burning because her fire glands have been removed. But you know they can wreak destruction without fire, especially if she finds a crown to rally." He waved his hand briskly to waylay any argument. "You're a guest here, Ba'Suon. You'll turn over your papers to me and when you go north to gather, you will round up the diamondback king that nests on the Jewel of the Crown Mountains. You will bring him to me and only then will I return your papers."

She stared at this Kattakan. That he would assume she was a gun for hire to do his bidding. "I will not."

He stood away from the desk. "Then you'll bide your time in my jail for releasing that dragon and Mr. Lilley will return to his employ with Volla."

Lilley said behind her, "She bought me out fair and square and hired me for the gather."

"That's not for you to decide."

"Volla's got her gold, Shearoji, and you got no cause to take away her permit, she's got more right to them dragons than you'll ever have."

She watched these two men combat with their eyes. They knew each other. Perhaps intimately. Lilley still sat, but every part of his body was drawn tense like fencing wire. She could refuse like he refused, but in this land she held no power they recognized and this Kattakan lord knew it.

He looked back at her. "For the journey to the mountains I will provide you three good horses that aren't afraid of dragons."

"Three?"

The lord called out. The inner door opened and the mustached man with the tight presence of a funeral veil stepped through. "My associate Raka will accompany you. You may find him indispensable since I hardly think a one-handed man would be of much use in the high country."

"Screw you, Tal," said Lilley. "I ain't ridin with him."

"You'll do as you're told or my jail is big enough for two."

Lilley scowled at this man named Raka, who seemed unmoved by the exchange. Raka was not a Kattakan name, but Ba'Suon. She scrutinized him. He looked past her. His coil of silence now pulsed toward her like the effect of sound without the notes of it. Behind the

Kattakan mustache she recognized certain planes of features that hadn't been clear before. The black of his eyes. His pistol sat in a brass-studded leather holster on his hip and his hand rested on the grip in a casual manner. He wore no blades. Other than his face there was nothing in his appearance that spoke of their common roots. Not even a hum of familiarity or tacit invitation to share his energy. This man was tightly enclosed within himself like a fist and she had never before felt such a thing from one of their own. Or at all. His vacant gaze chilled her bones and she drew a breath as armor against the vast emptiness suctioned around him.

"What is your family name?" she asked Raka.

"Your papers." Shearoji held out his hand. "Or my jail, Ba'Suon. I won't ask again."

She thought of the suon she had released and how she could call Cottontooth to her and raze this building from the suon's fighting strength alone. Raze this whole town. Lord Shearoji watched her thinking it. No one else made a sound.

She slowly retrieved the papers from her coat and held them out. He took them. It seemed to be a signal because then Raka walked past her and out the front door, his boots heavy on the wood floors, all the way across the porch and down the steps. The shadows on the street swallowed him and his death veil.

"He'll meet you at the livery stables in half of an hour," Shearoji said. And to Lilley: "Requisition some decent gear from Deswin. Tell him it's on my order."

Then Shearoji folded her papers in his large hands and left through the inner door, shutting it behind him.

The woman Volla seemed about to open her mouth to speak. Méka ignored her and quit the office all the way down the steps to the dirt track. Lilley followed her. "Where you goin?" he called.

She walked back to Shore Street and passed the grand hotel which was mainly a façade, and makeshift cafés and the gold office with a line up outside even at this hour. The sky was deep lavender and canopied by stars. The clouds had drifted away, revealing more of the moon's face and the box-like buildings limned by ghosts. She found a small structure with only a narrow door and two skinny dirt-scoured windows on either side, built of gray wood and set apart from the larger buildings. The flag of Mazemoor with its white chrysanthemum in the center hung above the door lintel in faded black and purple like discolored skin. Darkness behind the glass.

"You ain't gettin help from that quarter," Lilley said behind her.

She turned to him. He looked strangely sad. "It'll open in the morning."

"Won't make a difference. Shearoji's law runs this town and he's got validation all the way from the Fortress. You know the Fortress? In Diam? The High Lord of this country lives there in her big damn castle."

"Of course I've heard of the conqueror, but I broke no laws."

"Not accordin to Shearoji. They leave dragon matters to him, Méka. You'd be wastin your energy."

Her father had told her things would be different here than even he remembered, but he hadn't known this. The Greatmother of her family had said her dreams were the memories of the cosmos, and as such a part of her future. The golden land and the man doused in red.

"Who is Raka?"

Lilley blinked. "One of Shearoji's guns."

"But he's Ba'Suon."

"Your kind fought in the war right alongside people like the lord."

"Because we were promised citizenship and land." She thought of the woman in the saloon. She knew the reality of the stranded families. "We didn't believe in your war with Mazemoor. He's got no reason to stay on now."

"I reckon he's got at least one." Lilley rubbed his fingers together to indicate gold. The yellow poison.

She looked back at the Mazoön office. "Without my papers I have no defense here. And anything I do that's against the treaty with Mazemoor will be put on Mazemoor."

"He knows it. That's why he took em." Lilley gestured with his stump. "The Ba'Suon ain't free here, Méka. If they ain't makin you register to exist on the land, they're profiting off your skills. It's just the way it is. Are you gonna round up that dragon for him?"

She came here to gather. But not for gold and not for a Kattakan. She didn't answer, unsure whether her gold bought Lilley's loyalty like it did Raka's for Lord Shearoji, or if she was entirely surrounded by duplicitous Kattakans.

Lilley watched her for a moment longer, but seemed to decide something in himself. "I'd best be gettin my shit then. Can't march to the mountains in these rags. You're welcome to join me, might even have some chicory to drink."

THIS PERSON DESWIN lived in a shack on the outskirts of town toward the gold creeks. By the time they got there her boots were lathered in mud up to the shins. She waited outside a canvas-draped doorway as Lilley disappeared inside. Small wooden tables, a couple stools, and dented metal pots sat unwashed around the dregs of a dead fire. Inside, male voices molassed together, indistinct in tone. When Lilley emerged some minutes later, he wore layers of cotton, wool, fur and boots of Ba'Suon make, sturdy hide and bear pelt. He held a rifle and carried a riding satchel over his shoulder and a bedroll under his arm. A single pistol sat comfortably at his hip in a beaten holster. She remembered he'd been in the army. He knew the paths of the backcountry.

They spent some time rebuilding the fire. Once the flames were licking he set a pot of water to boil and greased a pan with pork fat and set it on a brazier above the fire. They sat on the low stools and watched it.

"Where do you sleep?" she asked. Shackled servitude was not a part of Mazoön culture, much less her own.

He nodded back toward the town. "Volla's got servant quarters. I won't be missin em. It's like livin with a hun'red others if you count all the bedbugs." After a minute, when the fat was bubbling, he laid out strips of smoked ham and on top of them a block of cheese, then unwrapped a muslin cloth of hard bread already broken into squares. He circled the bubbling center with two pieces on each side so they could soak up the grease. When all was melted and cooked enough he handed Méka a blunt knife so she could slice the bread and slip the dripping ham and cheese inside. This was a meal of riches and must have come from Deswin too. She didn't think a man who lived in servant quarters could afford such amenities.

Lilley ate and glanced up at the sky. Stars were falling along the western horizon. "So Cottontooth ain't gone for good?"

These Kattakans and their naming of free creatures. The pot bubbled so she wrapped the bread cloth around her hand and lifted it off its hook to set on the edge of the fire. Lilley offered her two tin cups with the chicory grounds spread inside and she poured in the hot water and gently shook each cup to stir the grounds around, then she handed him one of the cups. They sipped their drinks and it was almost a comfort, like sitting around the fire in one of her people's camps. But the muted life around her reminded her blatantly how much this wasn't a Ba'Suon camp. Only this odd Kattakan and his pulsing presence of *goldshard* and *redsun* seemed to occupy the edges of her senses. This Kattakan and his affinity for the suon.

i and sky and i
sister and i and goldcloud i

"She's north about a mile." Méka looked toward the mountains. "She won't go further."

"You can hear her."

Hear was what the Kattakans called it. It was better than trying to explain the sense of it. Or the suon's welcome of her, the acceptance as the suon saw fit. Méka nodded. "She's waiting for us. For me."

"Because you freed her?"

"Yes."

He shook his head and bit into the bread. Melted cheese dripped down his russet beard and he swiped at it with the back of his hand. "Years of dealin with your people and I still wonder at it."

"At what?"

"You and those dragons."

She chewed on the bread and looked at the windburn on his hand. "What do you know of gathering?"

"I know it's dangerous. Impossible for someone like me."

It would be. The complete immersion with the suon was something a Kattakan could not encompass, not even one as strange as Lilley. "I'll need you to head off the king if he tries to break. And curtail his crown if they intervene."

"Oh, just that? We only got one dragon."

"I'll get another on the mountain. I should be able to handle the king though. You can ride?" She meant the suon.

"Yeah." He stopped eating and paid his full attention to her.

"I can manage the rest. It's about connection, even with a diamondback. Connection through the most minute aspects of a suon's being. Dangerous, yes. Especially a diamondback of the north. Have you ever seen one?"

"Hell no."

"They're the largest of the king suon save for the ice suon of the arctic. This is why your Lord Shearoji wants him, most likely." For the pit. For the meat she'd seen selling in the pit dome. The thought alone soured the food in her stomach.

"He ain't my lord and I would prefer we leave them big boys alone."

"If there are too many kings competing for territory they can be destructive even to the land."

"And towns. I know. But are they even a threat to the land when the crowns've been decimated by my kind?"

She watched his eyes. It seemed to be an innocent question. "The Ba'Suon have also been decimated." By his kind. By the scattering he mentioned of families like the Sephihalé. "The suon still need to be gathered in the season."

He ate silently for a long moment. "If you ain't freed Cottontooth, how were you gonna round up?"

"I could cajole a wild one for the task, but one that is already akin to us makes it easier. It's a connection my people have forged with the suon for generations since these islands were young. The kings live longer under our care, the land thrives in their absence, the species propagates both wild and encamped. As do all other creatures beneath the wings of the suon."

He looked at her as if to gauge her reaction. "Then my people used em for war."

"Your people used many things for war. Bodies both suon and Ba'Suon. The land. One another."

"Don't that anger you?"

"If I let my anger run wild, it too would devastate everything in my path. And what of the world then?" She saw that he didn't understand. For a Kattakan, anger must always lead to retaliation. "Once we're in the air, you'll have to do exactly as I say."

"I sure as shit won't be kitin off on my own anywhere near a crown. Even if I was ridin a king myself." He began to chew on the bread again, pulling cheese like a fox tearing at gristled meat. "I never saw a gather, but I rode with your people into battle."

The scars on the piebald were tame compared to what the suon suffered in war with Mazemoor. The journey south with her family after the camps had been a somnolent march through eddies of mud and blood and some rampant shredding of flesh both human and suon. She remembered the stench as they passed through battlefields, the earth made crypt-like in its skeletal landscape and emaciated trees, the cloudy canopy of sky a mausoleum of encompassing grief. She'd held her brother's hand and wept for the sight witnessed by the stars, to be borne on the backs of their descendants. Refuge in Mazemoor did not soothe the mourning, and for a few moments staring into the flames of their cooking fire she smelled that odor of death once again.

"Tell me of your Sephihalé comrade. He taught you the suon?"

Lilley looked away and made a motion of his shoulder that was both shrug and agreement.

"Where is he now?"

"Gone. Like the rest of em." He cast his gaze to the dark outside their circle of fire. "Thanks to Raka."

"Raka?"

"Janan wanted to leave the army after the war and they wouldn't let him. Cause of his dragon. They wanted his dragon. They said if he tried to leave they'd kill him for desertion. Raka knew we planned to go and told Shearoji."

"Why would he do that?"

"Cause he's a traitor."

"But *why?*"

Something in Lilley's eyes hardened, some thought calcified and buried. But he only shrugged.

"Is that why you were in chains?"

He shifted on his seat and took another bite of the bread. As he chewed he seemed to think. "I helped Janan and his dragon escape, but I couldn't go with him. Shearoji was our superior. He said if I didn't wanna go to prison for it then I had to serve him. So then he gave me to Volla."

"Is that how you lost your hand?"

"Na, that was in battle. Mazoön dragonshot."

"So they didn't let any of the Ba'Suon soldiers go after the war, despite the accord."

"They let some of em go, just not the ones they

wanted to keep." His gaze found hers, flat as a shadow. The Ba'Suon were possessions to these Kattakans, if they weren't dispossessed altogether.

She thought of breaking into Shearoji's office to steal back her papers, but she was here by permission of the Mazoön government as much as the Kattakan one, and it had been clear when they'd issued her permit that she must abide by Kattakan law. To keep the peace. Their idea of peace, anyway, that didn't benefit those who'd had no say in the war in the first place.

The chicory turned bitter in her mouth. It might come to theft once she gathered the diamondback. Already she was resolved not to hand over the suon to the Kattakan lord. But any neat solution did not arise from the smoke of the cookfire to present itself to her knowing, so she could only contemplate the fantasy of rebellion.

Perhaps Lilley saw something in her expression. His voice sounded quieter. "It any better in Mazemoor? They welcome magic, don't they?"

She ate the last corner of her meal and looked at the breathing flames. "It's different."

"How?"

"They leave us alone."

"That's good then, ain't it?"

"It mightn't last too long."

"Why do you say that?"

She drank more of the chicory. "History. We share the same ancestors, but their ancestors drove out ours and that's how the Ba'Suon came to this land. They might decide to drive us out again."

He straightened back his shoulders. "I didn't know that."

She slung the remnant of her drink into the fire, awakening the burning tongues to hiss at her. "It was long before your people came to Ishia. Mazemoor was once called the world of the Ma'Suon. Just as this island is the world of the Ba'Suon. All of our islands, all of Ishia, are beneath the wings of the suon and the stars, with the long waters to bind us. Despite that map in Lord Shearoji's office, it will always be so."

THEY SET OUT toward the livery stables. As they walked Lilley loaded his rifle, pinching the stock between his arm and his ribs. With his single hand he fished the rounds out of his coat pocket to slide into the chamber. She watched him. He said, "What's he gonna do, arrest me?" The cheeky defiance drew a small smile from her and he returned it. But it faded once they came upon their new companion.

Three horses stood hitched to a post in the street, brushed and saddled. Raka lingered like a stone effigy by the tallest of them, a bay mare. He said, "You're late."

"You got a tryst to keep?" Lilley rounded a gray gelding and shoved his rifle into the saddle holster, his gaze on the Ba'Suon man over the back of his horse. "Nobody wants you here anyway, so you're welcome to stay in town."

As before, Raka's presence created a void in her

awareness. Being near him brought a precarious feeling to her stomach, like standing on the edge of a sinkhole. The horses shifted and shivered. They too felt it. Raka didn't look at her or reply to Lilley's words.

"We'll ride to the treeline," Méka said, "then make camp." The last horse was tall and black and swung its long head to look back at her as she ran her palm along his hindquarters. The round eyes rolled and nostrils flared. He must have scented suon on her clothes, but Shearoji had been correct, these horses remained steady, tolerant. She strapped her gear behind the saddle and did as Lilley had and armed her rifle. The black horse shifted his weight as she swung aboard and sat the rifle across her lap. She wrapped the reins in her fist and tapped the horse to turn him away from the stables. The two men fell in behind her and she led them on a path to the edge of town.

They rode on past the mud of trammeled ground and left the dim sporadic lights and ceaseless activity of Fortune City in their wake. Ahead in the bruised night, the land spread desolate as though victim to a barrage of suon fire or some fury of natural weather. Only two decades ago the ground of this valley had been carpeted with soft moss and bush, spring flowers and deep grass into which she remembered sinking her feet as a child. Further on the slopes, trees had once stood, the proud skirts of thick spruce, the elegant long legs of towering aspens whose golden leaves in the autumn shone brighter to her than anything these Kattakans mined beneath the earth. Her brother would chase her through the ghost pale trunks of birches, the whisper of their family connection melding with the hollow hiss of branches bent from a cooling breeze. Their mother would fashion peels of thin bark into bowls, and in the beginning of the Kattakan influx her people had traded such wares, long before even her grandparents' days.

Now nothing remained but inky mud and the detritus of churned gravel, results of a rapacious stratagem to unhinge the elements of the earth from itself. Ten years in a Kattakan camp and the world had decayed—not by natural recession but forced devastation. To look upon it had been to look upon the face of death and her family had made the decision to live beyond the reach of Kattakans. But it did not salve the mourn. Grief came to her anew and settled like a hawk upon her shoulders.

Instead of regal trees the horizon lay spiked with winch towers for hauling muck, bisected by hastily constructed flumes and sluice boxes to transport water and dirt. Interspersed in haphazard array, the raw log cabins and rain-smudged canvas tents housed numerous labor hands tasked to hack away at the bedrock for any speck of gold. Pinned to the edges of the camp were iron spikes driven into the ground and around them a handful of exhausted suon slept, shackled to the posts. Kattakans called them pay dirt dragons, diminishing their natural ability to detect gold and other precious metals to something serving only greed.

Méka and the men passed the sight, circumventing the spread of destruction. The enslaved suon raised their chins at her proximity. Nothing hummed, not even a murmur. Nature had laid itself down to die here and these creatures, surrounded by desolation and insult, could not even muster an echo of recognition.

Her heart strained and her vision blurred. She looked up at the glooming sky as they trod beneath it like specters pulled toward some semblance of an afterlife. The dead quiet compounded the sense of isolation, the Ba'Suon behind her on his bay mare a void into which nothing thrived. The mountains and foothills ahead were too far away for much beyond a distant, inconsistent sigh. She missed her people in the south, she missed how once they'd moved here in great camps, following the seasons and the stars. Though the Kattakan on his gray gelding gave off a subtle steady wave and sparks of *goldshard* and *dawnred*, like air troubled by the tossing of a sheet, his was not the familiar presence of a world connected to itself.

They rode on through land blighted by industry, crossed the footprints of the moon's light in single file. The horses' hooves stirred up rock dust and dead fires pulverized by the passing of iron cannons. The valley hardly stirred, as motionless as the sky, and the fetid stench of so much close living drifted like wraiths in their wake as if to call them back to exultant ruin. She knew they were clear of the toil when she felt the piebald cloud sail above them.

i and sky
i and gold and cloud
sister and i brother dawn
i and brother red and i

She looked up and the alabaster sheen of Cottontooth's scales flickered through the high atmosphere like an aurora. The whistling of the suon's passing sounded faint, but it was life, and she cast some knowing into the cool wind to offer of her presence. They were almost to the treeline on the edge of the valley when the suon descended into their path, the broad wings beating three times before talons sank into the earth and steadied her stance, hindquarters flexing as she took a step forward and dipped her long head down toward Méka.

i and sister and i

Her mount reared shallowly off the ground but she held it steady, rubbing its neck and guiding the horse's head to the side. She heard it blowing but as she rounded it broadside to the suon it settled. The other two horses wheeled under the hands of the men but similarly calmed, facing away as the cloud suon traced the air with her muzzle and flicked out an ashen tongue to taste. She would know horses, and with people aboard passed on them as prey not to be bothered, and lifted her angular head once more to scan the sky. Méka put out her hand, dropping the reins, and after a moment the suon dipped back to her, flaring white wings and unfurling her tail to score the shadows around them like brushstrokes of calligraphy. Méka spoke to her and stroked the tight panel of scales at her throat and for a few minutes the valley hummed with communion.

"We make camp here," Méka said.

WITH THE HORSES picketed and left to crop the low grass, they organized their bedding and Lilley set stones in a circle and gathered tinder and deadfall from the forest's edge to make a fire. Cottontooth walked a wide circuit around the camp and pissed into the scrub before settling some feet away from both the wet patch and the horses.

i and sleep and i

night and quiet and i

Raka lay with his head on his saddle and his hat resting over his eyes. His weapon belt lined along his side, but one hand rested upon it. A world unto himself with the globe of silence surrounding him and he seemed calm in the ether of it. Méka regarded him from the flank of the suon, across the loose circle of the camp, points of which they each had claimed with their gear for the rest of the night. Though she had not been able to see the man's face in her dream, the sense of disquiet about him felt much the same as with Raka. Greatmother said her dream would unfurl before her over time, like the land over which the people traversed season after season. That she needed to be here to find its path. She was not yet in a season of knowing the dream fully.

"Lilley says you fought with Lord Shearoji in the war," she said to Raka.

He didn't open his eyes or otherwise acknowledge that he had heard.

"Why do you barricade the world?" she said.

"He ain't gonna speak to you." Lilley knelt by the bed for their fire and began to build it, arranging the tinder to light then reaching into his pocket for a box of matchsticks. He struck one and set it to the tinder, then slowly began to stack the branches over the fire in a pyramid. He sat back on his heels and poked at the flames with the end of one of the deadfall sticks, his jaw winding in a chewing motion. The scent of licorice drifted on the air with the smoke. "He's too good for us, ain't that right, Raka?"

"Probably," said Raka.

"No dog of Shearoji's is too good for anythin."

Raka lifted his hat and looked at the other man. Lilley didn't look away. The fire cracked and spat.

Méka watched them. "If you're supposed to help me gather a suon for your boss but you won't touch the land, you're of no special use and I would do just as well with only Lilley."

Still no answer.

Lilley leaned back on his elbow and wagged his feet at the flames. "He's spyin on us for his master. Shearoji probably don't trust that you can do the job. Raka here's the only Ba'Suon he trusts and Shearoji's the only bastard that'll have anythin to do with him. His people don't even want him no more, not in town and not in the backcountry. It's a mystery for the ages when he's such a genial gent."

"Is that why you've severed from the world?" she said.

Raka lifted his hat from off his face and sat up. He put the hat on his head and gathered up his saddle and moved it away from the fire into the shadows and cold, then returned for his gear and his weapons and took them to the saddle far apart from them, the suon, and the warmth. Then he lay down again and placed the hat over his eyes and set his hand on his gun.

Cottontooth lifted her chin and followed after the man with her golden eyes. Her tail thumped the ground.

i and brother and rain

Even the suon understood Raka's sulk. Méka looked at Lilley and Lilley flicked his hand in dismissal as if he'd understood the suon.

"It's better this way."

THE DAWN EKED from the night in silver and rose with the sun pinned like a brooch on the hilly breast of the eastern horizon. When Méka opened her eyes, Raka stood by Cottontooth talking to her. He made no sound, nor did the suon, but Méka knew that he spoke to her in the way of their people because she felt the waves of it like a duet of fluting instruments trilling up and down the scales of knowing. All instinct and impression, not the symbols of verbal language. She didn't move, only listened. He stroked the suon's neck and up along her jawbone and trailed his fingers along the smooth ivory curve of her fangs. She curled her lips back as in a threat display but her eyes remained wide and her ears up, tail sliding along the soft grass behind her in slow curves like an eel slipping the surface of a lake. He pressed his cheek to her armored cheek and she chuffed twice. He moved then to her flank and stroked the spine of her wing so it lifted and arched over the camp, casting shadow. He ducked under it and held the edge-bone close to her ribs and stepped onto her haunch to swing himself up and across her back.

Méka sat up in her blanket, jostling the loose catch chains coiled beneath the saddle where she'd been lying. She watched as Cottontooth stood on her hindlegs and unfurled both wings and launched herself into the air.

Footsteps broke the ground from the treeline behind Méka, and Lilley said, "Is he stealin our dragon?"

"I don't know." She stood and picked up the rifle from beside her bedding. She sighted the circling white arrow as it ascended the cloud-stairs of the sky, tracking them with the barrel.

"You gonna shoot Cottontooth?"

"Him." She cocked the weapon. "If I have to."

But the trill of their conversation only twisted in more complicated patterns, underscored by the sound of air whistling through the suon's scales.

i and brother and sky red
wing i and cloud and brother and i

The rising sun seemed to add to the chorus with a bright ringing chime and the trees at the skirt of the mountains hummed and hissed. The clouds whispered like the wind and the air itself pattered in cadence until the dance of it all throbbed in her mind and behind her eyes so that she had to squint to follow their movements in the sky. She shook her head and attempted to sight them again but they flung like a kite, like a white scar across the pink and lavender flesh of the earth's bowl.

down

It was more direction than word, the feeling of falling that she cast out toward them, the hard grip of gravity to weigh on the buoyancy of flight. Cottontooth arched back as though pulled by an invisible bridle rein and then she straightened and arrowed straight toward the ground.

"Ware!" Lilley said.

The torrent of wind as the suon passed close overhead almost knocked them off their feet. In the next blink, Cottontooth descended to the ground from where she had launched. The wings beat and blew more breeze into their faces until the piebald cloud sat on her haunches and Raka stepped off her back and came toward Méka like a bullet.

She lowered her rifle. He caught the barrel and shoved it all the way down. She didn't resist but she stood solid and watched him as *no* and *stop* pummeled her chest. His silence broken.

Cottontooth swung her head around to stare at

them, eyes narrowed. *i and brother in storm* with a thump of her tail.

Méka tightened her grip on the weapon. Raka still held on, and for the first time he stared into her with such depth that she could also look back. But even with wide open eyes all the edges of him shadowed like a spilled silhouette over his corporeal form. Her breath contracted. Her eyes hurt. His stare attempted to gouge her right out of her body. Anger pulsed for a few moments more before she felt the caul drop once again around him and it heaved and tightened into that funeral veil. It seemed to blur his features for a moment, and when she blinked and looked again he was that void extending out like it was itself gathering breath into some energetic lungs. She stood in the hollow of it but had no awareness that she was standing at all.

"Don't ever do that again." His deadened voice broke the thick absence and the sky suddenly clamored overhead in swathes of burning colors, racketing against her ears. But if any life touched him at all, he didn't show it. He shoved the rifle into her chest and let go.

She staggered a breath and held the weapon tightly. "Why did you ride her?"

Lilley came up to her left side, a hand on his sidearm, a flare of *bloodhot* emanating toward Raka as strong as any Ba'Suon presence. But she held out her arm to stop his advance.

i and cloud gold and i brother storm
soft sky and i

The suon was no worse for the ride and rose to her feet to stand behind Lilley, her wing arching over them all. But Méka tried to discern some sense in Raka beyond the creature's reassurance and got none.

Raka stared at her only, the scorched regard of molten earth. "If you want my help with the diamondback, stay out of my way."

His presumption reeked of Kattakan logic. "I directed myself to the suon, not to you."

"She's not yours to direct."

"Nor is she yours to ride. I didn't ask for your help," she said, but he was already walking back toward his bedroll far from their dead fire. Her hands flexed around the rifle stock as she tracked his actions.

"What the fuck was that about?" said Lilley.

She still watched the Ba'Suon man. He was packing up his gear with swift, purposeful movements. She watched him check the ammunition in his gun. So he could be agitated after all. He could feel anger, even possessiveness. And briefly, in those moments in communion with the suon—he could feel free. He was not just the void.

"It's light enough," she said. "Let's get on."

LILLEY RODE UP alongside her when they were well into the morning and deep inside the bristling trees, which cast a perpetual dusk across the forest floor. He glanced over his shoulder to where Raka rode a dozen yards behind. The suon had flown out of sight, but

Méka felt her some distance away, carving high circles against the canopy of the sky. Hunting.

"What do you think he's about?" Lilley said. "As one of your people. Janan used to always tell me to be kinder to him, but look where it got him."

"Raka?"

"Janan. Look where it got him, the fucker betrayed him anyway."

She looked across at Lilley. "He's more than he's saying."

"He ain't sayin nothin."

"I don't know that he's Shearoji's man."

"Why do you say that?"

"He may be with your people, but he still feels in the manner of our people."

"Cause he rode Cottontooth?"

She remembered the symphony of it. "The way he rode her."

"How did he ride her?"

"Effortlessly," was the only way a Kattakan could understand.

"She ain't wild. And he was in the war with em. Same as Janan."

"I can't explain it to you." She motioned with her chin. "Ride on ahead a little."

"Why?"

"Because I'm going to speak to him and you only seem to aggravate each other."

Lilley huffed a breath, but he touched his heels to his horse and they picked their way forward, stirring dead needles and leaves and earth. She reined her horse and waited for Raka to catch up until his silence wrapped around them both. Even the trees fell still in his passage. Their stirrups bumped together and he surged his mount enough to avoid her. She caught up again.

He looked straight ahead. "What."

"You know what."

"I don't owe you words, sister."

"So you recognize I'm your sister, Ba'Suonsha." He didn't answer or react to the term of endearment. "What is your family name?"

"I know you." Now he glanced at her, half a tilt of his chin and the sharp edge of his dark eyes. "Suonkang. I recognize your blades. Only a Suonkang would come this far north to gather a king."

She looked down at her blades as they sat on the belt around her hips. The carved suon tooth and ebony scale. "So you aren't so exiled from our people that you forget."

"All Ba'Suon remember the families who refused Kattaka and fled to their enemies."

"The Mazoön aren't *our* enemies. They rise from these islands same as we do."

He didn't reply.

"Did your family remain here or just you?"

"Tell me, is Mazemoor the sanctuary you thought it would be?"

Her horse shook its mane and snorted. At the heels of the blue and white trees, small animals scampered as they passed.

"They aren't so bold as Kattaka in how they wish to use us," she said, "but at least in order to live our lives fully we aren't forced to work for them."

"So the families move about freely in the south."

"More or less, yes. The Mazoön call their 'magic' superior but they acknowledge our ways. We aren't compelled to fit them with suon or enlist in their army for recognition."

They rode on in silence, the hollow of their words falling to nothing. Even her own breath muted in her ears, her blood not even a murmur in witness to the life she possessed. But he didn't push away from her this time and, despite the fact he wouldn't look at her, something of a strange companionship seemed to glimmer in the fog.

She looked at him. "Do none of the Ba'Suon in town cross your paths?"

He didn't answer, perhaps didn't need to. His kind of silence also meant solitude, and any Ba'Suon would want to steer clear of his funereal presence. Except, apparently, Sephihalé ele Janan.

Raka gestured to the forest. Beyond the trees and even the mountains. "You ever think about if the families had organized and resisted the Kattakans, we could all still be crossing paths in our ancestral lands?"

"And how many would have died?"

"Mostly their people."

"And the land in the ensuing scourge. The suon even more. That isn't our way. Why do you work for Lord Shearoji if you think of resisting the Kattakans?"

He looked toward her, but past her shoulders. The glimmer in the fog snuffed out. "Ride to your red-haired slave."

She nudged her horse forward. "There are no slaves here, Ba'Suonsha ele Raka."

He didn't like the diminutive; for a moment the disdain speckled her back like hail. But it was like light once again slanting from the sinkhole of his kinetic absence. "That isn't my name."

"It is until you release your born one," she said over her shoulder.

Lilley dropped back to meet her and gestured to the suggestion of a path through the bone-wrought trees. "It's only gonna get thicker, but I know a different way from where your people cut a trail."

They rode on well into the sun's peak and stopped for food in a small clearing where evidence of her people lay imprinted in the ground from generations of resting through journeys. The field spread only as wide as five sheltering mata clustered in circles as in her family's camp, or any camp of her people from here to the southern isles. Cottontooth descended from the blue sky in a gust of air and promptly staked out the center of the clearing by pissing on the wild grass. A scent like burnt metal permeated the air, announcing the piebald's presence and warding off any other creatures in the area—suon or otherwise. Battle-wrought she might have been, but she didn't forget generations of living amongst the Ba'Suon.

Lilley rubbed his neckerchief across his nose and

got down from his horse to tether it to a low branch. Cottontooth swung her long neck and peered at the prey animal, but Lilley approached her to stroke her cheek and block her sight of the horse, clicking at her with affection. *goldcloud* shimmered over the field in a slow wave. For a moment Méka saw her dream in a wisp at the corners of her eyes, but without the sense of foreboding. In a blink the image disappeared and instead the only gold was the stare of the suon.

i and brother and i
nettle and night

Méka looked across at Raka before climbing down from her mount. "Running off, or will you stay?" He'd come alive with the suon, he might yearn for it still. Surely he felt her recognition of him.

But he didn't reply, just unhitched his canteen from the saddle and disappeared amongst the trees.

Lilley looked at her like she should have known the answer and fished out a biscuit from his saddle pack. "You know the oldest horse that ever lived was seventy years old?"

Cottontooth dipped her chin and plucked the Kattakan's hat right off his head with her teeth. She straightened back to avoid his grabbing hand and he gave up after a few swipes.

Méka smiled. "Was it a Ba'Suon horse?"

"Na. Why? Do you magic your animals?"

"Not in the manner you mean." She moved to Cottontooth and held out her hand. The suon handed her the hat and dropped her head to crop at a dwarf bush. Méka touched the spine of her left wing. The tail coiled and unfurled slowly in response. When she looked at Lilley he was watching her with an unreadable expression. "Here's your hat." She held it out.

He set it far back on his forehead so his vision wasn't obstructed. "Been a long time since I seen a Ba'Suon handle a dragon like you." There was a shadow of sadness in his voice.

"Sephihalé ele Janan?"

He nodded.

She considered prying for more history—there were yet untold facets about this strange Kattakan to discover—but the shadow passed out of his countenance when Cottontooth slid the end of her tail around his ankles so he had to step over it not to trip. Like a game they often played.

"Where was this old horse?" Méka said.

"It was brought from mainland Kattaka over a century ago, so it's probably bullshit. But Janan said he'd heard about it from his grandfather, and so on goin back in his family."

"Then it must be true. Some people have lived for more than a hundred years."

"Ba'Suon?"

"Yes. But others too."

Lilley lifted his hat and wiped the leathered wrist of his absent hand across his forehead. Despite the mountain air, the sun beat perspiration from his pale skin. He swatted at tiny black flies that flitted around his face and reset his hat. "That's old as shit. I reckon you can't do much if you're a hun'red."

"Could the horse still move?"

"The legend says it went into battle and died there, not of old age."

"We're energetic creatures by nature. Some possess a better hold on that energy."

"That's how it all works, yeah?" Lilley looked up at the sky and all around at the trees, the clearing. "Janan said that's how the Ba'Suon get on with things. You feel how the world's made and it can feel you."

"That's as good an explanation as any."

"Why do you think it's just the Ba'Suon and not someone like me?"

She ran her hand along the pearlescent paneling of the cloud's throat. Cottontooth made a soft sound through her fangs and Méka understood suddenly the nature of Lilley's name for her. "You're a little different. I don't know why. The stars see you differently."

He blinked. "See me?"

"You are..." *goldshard* She looked at him. *bloodred* But he didn't react at all to the impression, somehow existing as a nucleus but ignorant of his own orbit of light. "Perhaps it's from knowing Sephihalé ele Janan. And the suon, through him." She couldn't fully understand what it meant for one of her own to go to war and fight alongside Kattakans, what energy was exchanged in the evisceration of battle, how the stars absorbed the strife and the care. They must have become a family unto themselves, formed in blood.

"Was Raka in your unit?"

Lilley looked toward the trees as Raka stepped into view. "Like a conjured demon."

"There's a pond down that way." Raka gestured behind him. "We oughtta water the horses."

"Ever heard of the seventy-year-old horse?" Lilley asked Raka. It didn't sound like an idle question.

"Are you still going on about that damn horse?"

"Janan told Raka the story too, didn't he, Raka? You remember that time around the camp at Fort Nemiha. Tell Méka if you were in my unit durin the war, she was askin."

She studied the other Ba'Suon as he joined her beside Cottontooth. He still didn't look at her, but despite his closed nature he was drawn to the suon, like any Ba'Suon. Cottontooth stretched out a foreleg and flexed her talons and Raka dutifully stroked roughly along the muscled panel of pale scales.

"You keep your mouth open so much and something's bound to fly in," he said to the Kattakan.

"You threatening me?"

"It's not a threat to point out our mutual understanding of nature and black flies."

"He's a real good killer," Lilley said with pointed clarity, though Raka now turned toward his horse and ignored them both. "Makes you wonder, don't it."

Méka watched him step aboard his mount and pat its neck. His violence didn't feel driven. Not even in that moment after his flight on Cottontooth—that anger had been seated in fear.

* * *

THE WEATHER DIDN'T hold. As they climbed further up the flank of the mountain the sun disappeared and the first smatters of rain sliced through the canopy and began to soak the forest floor. Méka pulled her hood up over her head and the men stopped to unpack oiled slickers to loop around their shoulders and drape over their hands. Nobody spoke as they followed her through the afternoon gloom and on toward the evening. They ate in their saddles and that night remained chill and wet. They slept beneath stunted trees and rose at the first blink of dawn, when the rain had abated only slightly. She attempted to rally their day by asking Raka about his mustache. Teasing was a strong part of their culture and surely he would respond in some manner. "Is it to blend in with the Kattakans? You should shave it now, Lilley and I don't care."

"But it took him a whole year to grow that thing," said Lilley.

They got no response and she began to suspect it had less to do with his lack of interest and more from a stubborn pride. To break up the mood Lilley produced a harmonica from his pocket and rang some bending tunes over the alpine shoulders near and far. Hundreds of feet above, Cottontooth sang back in throaty ululation. Lilley was surprisingly good despite the cacophonous accompaniment, and not even Raka complained. They chattered little and then mostly about practical considerations.

By mid-afternoon a little sun swept its rays across the sky, but it was short-lived. Picking their way parallel to a steep drop-off into the heads of dwarf trees, Lilley gestured down the muddy slope and called back in their single-file line. "You know where we at, Raka?" Raka, bringing up the rear of their small posse, didn't answer. Lilley spoke to the dim path ahead but his voice dragged behind him like a sledge. The words seemed to carve lines in the ground as Méka peered into the tumble and rot of foliage. "That down there's a mass grave of horses and people and one or two dragons. Not from the war."

The cold air crawled inside the collar of her coat. Indeed, there bubbled some black mass from those shadows. Not the absence of being that rode behind her, but the lingering of living things that had been flayed from their quickened existence and hidden from the gaze of the stars. "From what then?"

"Pioneers on a perilous journey," Lilley said. "Bold enough to bull their way up the Crown with only a single guide. Tell her the rest, Raka."

Again only silence.

"Our talkative companion here was their guide. Then somethin or other about a storm and the whole company slid down that gully. Somehow our boy Raka survived."

Méka turned in her saddle and looked at the Ba'Suon man. Even staring straight at him elicited no reaction on any plane of awareness. Above them the piebald cloud called out, sounding the environment for other suon. Raka tilted back his chin to gaze up through the trees, brought to life only by a language older than his own.

THEY WERE BOUND to cross paths with a Ba'Suon camp and on their third day riding through the hills she felt the orchestra of a family mata staked by a mountain stream. The prospect of a generous fire and warm food propelled their pace until they broke from the trees and spied the round paint-patterned shelters arranged in concentricity throughout a wide clearing. A cordon of five young suon sat outside the largest mata. On the other side of the camp stood a small pen of goats and fowl and a picket of four sturdy horses. It was late afternoon and the rain drizzled haphazardly at slants across their faces. They didn't have to say a word—before they could even dismount, the matriarch of the family emerged from the large mata and hailed them in a sharp eastern dialect. Méka gave her family name. The Greatmother's charcoal-rimmed eyes moved from Lilley to Raka and back to Méka before she disappeared inside the mata.

"We all right?" Lilley said, his voice hoarse from lack of use in the last few cold hours.

"Yes. This is the camp of the family Lapliang. Would you tend to the horses?"

Two youths ducked from one of the smaller mata and approached to help. Lilley nodded up and greeted them in the dialect of the family Sephihalé, which surprised the boy and girl. He asked them if they knew of the seventy-year-old horse. When Méka looked back around, Raka was nowhere, though his horse remained, its reins now caught in the boy's hand. She cast her knowing out toward the trees to follow the dearth of life that he engendered, like looking into a great abyss, but Lilley stepped into her line of sight, emanating *redsun*.

i and i family and
sky and night
fire and meat and i

"Let him go," said Lilley, as Cottontooth whirled overhead, her wings a drum of joy. "You chase him down and he's only gonna dig in his heels further. Then it'll take a dragon's jaws to uproot even a glimmer of his sense."

"I could use the help in talking to him and you already have a rapport."

"That ain't what I'd call it. You said yourself we aggravate each other."

She tested a thought. "You haven't always been angry with him."

Lilley stared at her, rain mist dotting his shadowed features.

"Will you speak, or are we to stand here in the wet indefinitely?"

"I ain't of the mind to, na."

She showed him her teeth and turned away. "I had to be saddled with the most contrary men in both our lands."

Inside the large mata a pot of goat stew boiled in the center of the canvas floor. A welcome warmth that spoke of solace. Méka heeled off her boots at the door and set her gear against one of the walls beside a couple of brightly painted buckets and began to unload the catch chains and weapons and coat from off her body. Divested of all encumbrances, she raised her hands upward to shoulder height, palms to sky, in greeting to the family and to the cosmos. The matriarch and nine Lapliang of all ages sat around the stovepot. Occasionally a young man with red suon scales in his braids stirred it and added herbs and vegetables in intervals while the smoke sailed up toward hand-holes in the ceiling. Méka walked over the flower-woven rug and knelt across from the matriarch, whose presence undulated outward to all the camp in calm, fat waves. Her skull was lightly bristled with white hair and beneath it were faint remnants of her youthful tattoos, the geometric shapes covering most of her head and down the sides of her neck. Telling a life.

"Thank you, Greatmother." Méka retrieved a silk sachet from her shirt pocket and offered it with both hands. The old woman accepted it and opened it to reveal the chrysanthemum buds, southern sunberries, and blooms of honeysuckle. She nodded in approval, rewrapped the small bundle and handed it to one of the older men whose wrinkled face spoke of years of smiles. The ornateness of his braids and multicolored suon scales gave him a bird-like mien. He moved to a small iron pot already boiling beside the stew and tossed the offering in to steep the tea.

"You're far from your current paths, Suonkang," said Greatmother.

"It's so. I'm heading up the Crown to gather for my family."

"With that Kattakan and the lost one?"

"The lost one?"

"The one who refuses to come into camp."

Méka peered into the dark eyes, slightly rimmed around the iris by a milky ring. "Do you know him?"

"I've never seen him with my eyes, but I know." Greatmother gestured around the mata but she meant the mountain. "He's from the north. The far north. The dead family Abhvihin."

Even the air outside seemed to stop moving. The red wooden door of the mata creaked as if someone had stepped over the threshold, but there was nobody.

"You know the family?" said Greatmother.

"All Ba'Suon know of the family Abhvihin. We heard of it even in the camps." She couldn't fathom the loss. "But we thought the son had also perished."

Greatmother nodded once. "Perhaps he wishes he had and that's why he dwells among the Kattakans. Being around a family is perhaps too much of a reminder."

"His silence then. He's protecting his pain."

"He tries. But if he's accompanying you up the mountain, you should take care of him. For his own balance and the balance of the world."

Her own Greatmother of the Suonkang had said a similar thing. But she had been speaking of the dream.

Land ablaze with light and always this man in the distance, his back to her. "How can I help him when he blocks me out?"

Greatmother spread her hands. "I can't tell you that. Maybe he will."

The old man tending to the tea ladled the steaming liquid into small ceramic cups for all occupants of the mata. He offered to Greatmother first, then to Méka, who accepted it with both hands and a nod of thanks. The sweet floral drink warmed her through when her body had chilled despite the stove heat. As she sipped she tried to sound through the trees for the presence— or absence—of the Ba'Suon with whom she had traveled for three days now. But he must have been far away or locked so efficiently within himself that she could not discern him from the natural movement of air and sky, or the particles within.

"How do you come to know him?" asked Greatmother.

"He was ordered to accompany us by Lord Shearoji of Fortune City. I had no choice."

"The stars deem it then."

The door slammed open on a gust of wind and Lilley ducked through, the blast of his *goldshard* preceding him by a single breath. "My apologies." He closed the door behind him with more care and, like Méka, began to remove his gear, guns, and outer clothing. Lastly he sat on a low bench near the mata wall and yanked off his boots one at a time, then gestured briefly in the manner of the Ba'Suon, to Greatmother and to the cosmos, and joined Méka on the woven rug, legs crossed. The old man offered him the tea and he took it with thanks and sipped. His dark red hair lay pasted to his forehead like streaks of blood and he passed his handless wrist across the waves. The leather came away damp. He smelled of horse and rain but Méka found it strangely comforting. The grounding of the earth when her mind kept bending toward thoughts of the dead and the destroyer among them. One of her own.

They all drank tea in silence, as if the presence of the Kattakan cast a contemplative mood upon them all. A young girl stood from the opposite corner of the stove and came around to pass them hot wet cloths so they might clean their faces and hands. Greatmother seemed to brighten as the old man retrieved all of their cups and poured them a second round of the tea.

Lilley gestured to the goat stew. "That smells delicious, ma'am." He spoke in the Sephihalé dialect, meeting the venerable woman's eyes.

She regarded him plainly. "You were in the war?"

"Yes ma'am."

"No need to call me ma'am."

"Yes ma'am."

The corners of her eyes wrinkled more. "What is your name?"

"Lilley."

"What a pretty name for a pretty man," Greatmother said, flirtation curving her lips.

Lilley smiled back. "Thank you, ma'am."

"You speak well in the dialect. Learned in the war?"

"After a manner. Do you know the family Sephihalé?"

"I do."

"I learned from one of their sons. We fought together." He looked into his cup and sipped his second pour of tea down to the buds and berries.

"I had heard Sephihalé ele Janan went south to Mazemoor after the war."

Lilley's gaze lifted and sharpened. "So he did." He cleared his throat. "How'd you know that's who I meant?"

"We crossed paths with the remnant of his family in this land. Many of us know of the suon soldier who fell in love with the red and gold Kattakan."

Méka looked at her companion. It seemed the intricacies of his relationship with Raka weren't the only aspects of this peculiar Kattakan. The strong impression of the family Sephihalé in Lilley now made more sense. In the firelamps of the mata his skin rose to a heightened pink.

Greatmother smiled with fondness. "The stew is ready."

They drank warm goat's milk sweetened with honey and soaked biscuits in the stew, sitting around the hearth and talking of the weather to come and their paths through the mountains. Méka consulted with one of the Lapliang trackers, while Lilley chimed in with all he remembered about the behavior of the range. The information filled in the gaps of what had changed since the last time a Suonkang had traversed these heights almost two years ago.

Outside, the suon bellowed occasionally into the evening sky and the goats seemed to answer back with their feeble brays. Throughout the supper, more of Greatmother's family joined them in the big mata until the space grew crowded with the scent of all the bodies and their tobacco and the heat. One of the young men lifted down an ornately painted three-string guitar from the wall and began to play it with expert, nimble fingers. The high bending notes slung through the air and Lilley took out his harmonica and joined in, much to the whole mata's delight. The old man sat a skin drum between his knees and kept cadence, mimicking the beat of a suon's wings. Greatmother clapped her hands and a couple of the children began to wheel ungainly around the floor. One of the girls caught Méka's hand and urged her to her feet, so Méka locked fingers with her and danced around the central mata poles.

In the whirling she didn't notice Lilley had jumped in. He had given up the harmonica to a woman who blew into it with discordant abandon. He caught Méka's hand, their calluses pressed together. The roughened warmth of his grip seemed to bolt an energetic shard straight through her midsection. Perhaps he felt it. Gone was the reticence of earlier. His smile was wide in a way she had never noticed, his teeth an inconsistent mix of sharp baby fangs and two larger, blunt front teeth, as if he hadn't quite grown into an adult bearing. Some supple, gilded part of him glittered in her mind's eye and she thought she caught the dust of it streaked through his red hair and beard, transforming him into some creature of fire and light. The muted caul of tension that had followed them up the mountain disintegrated in the revelry and buoyancy of all the Ba'Suon in this mata. Arrows of merriment struck out to the horses, the livestock, the suon and the mountainside itself, moving in currents through the running stream and forking between tree branches until even the canopy seemed to cavort in the edges of her knowing. A few of the children began to sing, their clear, sweet voices an evocation of the air through the scales of a suon in flight.

If it were possible she would have stretched this feeling far to the south so her family in Mazemoor could feel it, so they could know that she found connection in their ancestral paths once again despite the fleeing from them, and though their people were spread across the islands now, the earth and other families of the Ba'Suon here had not forgotten or forsaken them. All stood in balance under the stars and forever would it be so.

Or almost all. Exhausted from both dance and laughter, she asked to fill a bowl of the stew to take to Raka. Greatmother gestured her agreement. "If you can find him." But Méka sent a silent call to Cottontooth instead and let the warmth in her belly exude out toward the deep blue sky streaked by the cloud of the cosmos. By and by the broad white wings shuttered the stars and Cottontooth alighted on the grass near to the camp's suon. For some minutes all of them chuffed and hissed at one another in some display of territorial debate. Raka stepped down from the cloud's shoulders, took the stew and walked off into the trees. Méka followed him.

"Greatmother told me about your family," she said to his back where he stood eating and facing the skeletal night.

He kept on eating.

"How did it happen exactly?"

The sound of the spoon on the inside of the bowl ceased for a minute. His chin turned but he didn't face her. "I don't owe you my memories."

"I think you do. You're riding with us. You're supposed to help me gather a king. How do I know you won't bring down the whole mountain on our heads?"

"I won't."

"Was it truly a storm that killed those pioneers?"

His voice emptied out like the words were only a sieve. "Leave me alone, Suonkang."

She took a step closer. She thought of the piebald suon and *softscale*. The stroke of a hand on a wing. Nearby Cottontooth felt it and *i and brother falling and i* echoed toward them. She watched his body breathe. "How did it happen, Abhvihin ele Raka?"

He flung the dregs of the stew at the trunks of the trees and turned around. He came toward her and pushed the bowl against her chest. "Thanks for the food," and kept walking to the suon.

"I'm not letting you ride her. She'll stay in the camp for the night."

That drew his full attention, half-obscured in shadow. But it didn't matter; the void of him pressed against her. "Not *let* me?"

She took a step closer. "I don't know if you're safe, so you aren't riding her."

"She's safe."

"With you?"

"She's safer now than where she was in that pit with Lilley."

"That's hardly difficult. Tell me why she's safer with Abhvihin ele Raka of the once great family of the far north." She watched how his eyes were illuminated by moonlight and the summer night, how they cast a spectral stare at all he looked upon. "I just want to understand, Raka. We're both born of this land, or do you hate us so much? Me, Janan, this camp that offers you food and shelter even knowing the fate of your family? Stop turning us away."

He sniffed, reaction to the cold or some impulse of impatience. He swiped the rough sleeve of his coat across his mouth. "I was a child. I didn't have the control. I didn't know what I had, and neither did our Greatmother. Nobody knew." Even now, in just that confession, she felt the bars lock tighter around him like iron gates. "So it all came out as destruction."

"Destruction in and of itself isn't against our nature. You aren't at fault."

He stared at her, the pulse of a brewing anger. "You say this to me?"

"Nature itself is both destruction and renewal. That

is the balance. That's what our people are all born with to varying degrees. Surely your Greatmother understood this."

"There's nothing to be done if it's all storm and tidal waves."

"Nothing of nature is *all* storm. Especially not people. But try to hold back a storm and what eventually happens?"

He gave her the edge of his shoulder, scanning the dark.

"I feel these barricades in you but they won't hold, Raka."

"They've held all my life since that day, Suonkang."

"All the more reason to expect another deluge."

"You don't know what you're talking about. And you certainly don't have solutions. So leave me be. I'll meet up with you when you ride out tomorrow."

"What did you do to Sephihalé ele Janan?"

"Surely that Kattakan told you."

"Lilley says you betrayed him to Shearoji."

"Then that's what I did."

"Why won't you account for yourself, Raka?"

Now he looked back at her, but his eyes were hidden. "What difference would that make? They'd all still be dead. You reckon words will drop my family whole from the stars?"

He might as well have extinguished the sky and the world with it. She wanted to take hold of his arms, touch his face, remind him he wasn't lost. Had Janan tried too?

But in the end he left her alone in the dark, separating himself from the warmth of the camp.

GREATMOTHER LODGED HER and Lilley in a corner of the big mata where two narrow beds braced against a wide hanging tapestry of ornate orange, blue, and black diamond pattern. They were a little drunk, as the old man had broken out casks of honeyed liquor bought at lowland Kattakan markets and she'd allowed herself to be cajoled to empty the cups. Tomorrow they would set out again, and Raka would be as Raka was, but tonight was for family and laughter under the bosom of the sky. Greatmother asked her only once if Abhvihin had enjoyed the stew.

Now she lay listening to Greatmother snoring on the opposite side of the mata.

Lilley wasn't asleep. "Where you think Raka's gone?" he whispered across the small space between the bows of the beds.

So the man cared, or at least enough to wonder if their back was protected.

"Oh, you want to talk now?" she said, hoping he took her teasing for a serious gripe.

He made a snuffling sound into the bedding, like a dog settling in for sleep. "Don't you ever got things you don't wanna make real by speakin em aloud?"

"Not speaking of something doesn't make it any less alive."

"Talkin about it don't help it neither."

"You're more like Raka than you want to admit."

He grunted with disgust. "I'd sooner shoot him than stand next to him."

"That's why you want to know where he went?"

"In my experience it's best to keep him in your sight, if you gotta keep him at all."

Méka stared up at the wooden ribcage of the mata, now shrouded in shadows like the ash leavings of long-ago cave paintings. "He's somewhere he can be alone." She hadn't felt Cottontooth leave.

"Reckon he'll come back?"

"Where would he go otherwise?" Not back to their people where it was difficult to forget what he'd done. And he couldn't return to Lord Shearoji empty-handed. "You need to know something about Raka if he's to join us to the Jewel."

"What?"

"It's known among my people that he killed his entire family."

"*What?*"

So Sephihalé ele Janan hadn't told this to his lover. "There was once a great family of the Ba'Suon whose paths crossed the far north. A fierce family who harnessed the cold and gathered the ice suon of the deep glaciers. Sometimes, but not often, their paths crossed to these lands for trade. Even amongst the greatest families of the southern Ba'Suon they were an intimidating people. They never traded with Kattakans, so many of your people assumed they were myth or long extinct."

She heard him breathe out slow. "It's hard to believe anybody could survive that far in the cold. They say even your spit freezes before it hits the ground."

"It's so. But the family of the far north all stopped because of Raka. He didn't intend to kill them but his knowing is unstable. I had thought it strange that he couldn't... that I couldn't 'see' him. There is a way that we understand the world and all natural elements within it. Including one another. There's a way that we see and feel things down to the smallest, most invisible elements. Raka feels set apart and it's a very wrong feeling."

"Is that what you meant by how he barricades himself?"

"Yes."

Lilley fell silent. Méka could almost reach out her hand and touch the curiosity and fear rippling out from him.

"If he's unstable," said Lilley, "then what's he doin with Shearoji? How did he fight in the war and not obliterate the entire island? And what if he goes berserk with us?"

"All good questions. I can only assume by removing himself from his people he's managed to tether himself somehow. At least to live with some capacity of control."

"Some."

She would not tell the Kattakan soldier that control and suppression were opposed conditions, and she thought that Raka operated on the latter. "I believe Janan understood this in him and desired to help him. *I* need to help him. He's in pain, and for the Ba'Suon this makes an unbalanced world."

The dark held Lilley's thoughts for some time. "You gotta be careful, Méka."

She knew so. But the true concern in his tone filtered some warmth between them and softened the conversation. "Sleep now. We have long days ahead of us."

"With any luck." She heard him roll over but instead of settling into slumber he reached out to her in the shadows and touched the edge of her bedframe. "I never, uh, thanked you for buyin me out."

"There's no need."

"Yeah there is. A man without freedom's hardly a man at all. Just like Cottontooth was hardly her nature when she was used in the pit. I reckon you understand that as a Ba'Suon of this land." He paused. "Hazhka, Suonkang ele Mékahalé."

"Pesh'dewa," she said. And, a little quieter, "Lilleysha."

THE SUON WOKE them with the dawn. She caught the first burnished glimmers of light and sound as Lilley ducked through the door, bringing with him the pointed squabble of the small crown outside. She thought she recognized Cottontooth's voice bullying the domesticated ones.

"They sure can stare at you when you're takin a leak." He gestured to the door as Méka sat up to breathe deeper and draw some semblance of alertness into her blood. "We better get a move on while the weather's good."

The camp was already awake. Greatmother had let her sleep, a rare gift to a guest. The family sat around an outdoor fire with cups of tea and pans of cured fish and salt bread. Méka and Lilley joined them and ate with thanks, the motions of the morning a familiar jumble as children ran back and forth, animals grunted and called, and the adults talked of coming weather and gossip from other families recently met. One of the wranglers asked Méka about the Suonkang camp in Mazemoor and she recounted some memories of fishing at a mountain lake similar to the one here, and how the northern suon like the piebald cloud grew twice as large as the ones found in the south. Her family had to be extra diligent in the areas in which they encamped so as not to imbalance the surrounding nature. As she spoke, images of her parents and brother conjured like revenants around the fire, her brother braiding their father's hair with suon scales and their mother sharpening her blades. The scent of wood ash and green twice as acute as, season by season, persistent life slowly worked to supplant the years of Kattakan camps. Of log buildings and guards and signed papers promising peace. Now, as she looked on the Lapliang faces, a family only a quarter in size of what it should have been, she wondered if there had been any peace at all. Where was the new growth, and was the measure of not going to war simply survival?

Her Greatmother said the world and the stars moved in long cycles, and decisions made for hasty needs garnered only temporary futures. War was a corruption of all of nature and the thought of it alone tightened a fist in the center of her chest. But so did the sight of a suon in a fighting pit. She didn't speak of these things, it would interrupt the lightness she felt in the Lapliangs, but she sensed Lilley watching the side of her face and turned to meet it. His eyes soaked up the gray morning, wide and wondering. Was her mood so obvious to this Kattakan? Nearby Cottontooth trilled, muzzle cast to the sky. *í aŋd day wíŋg í*

When she and Lilley returned to the big mata to pack their gear, one of the young women trailed behind and tugged on Lilley's sleeve. Méka recognized her as the wrangler who'd jubilantly but inexpertly played Lilley's harmonica last night. Now she presented the Kattakan with a necklace of red and gold suon scales. Lilley's brows rose in surprise and his smile eased across his face in genuine appreciation.

"Hazkha, allasha," he said repeatedly.

Being called little sister seemed to make the woman blush. More so when Lilley took out the harmonica from his pocket and offered it to her. They said many thanks to each other and held each other's hand with the individual gifts locked between them before the wrangler departed the mata, clutching the harmonica to her belly. Lilley draped the necklace so it fell midway down his chest and touched the hard, oval shapes of the scales. The gold shone like the nuggets mined so ardently outside Fortune City. The red ones were like garnets. After a moment of thought he tucked the necklace inside his shirt.

"So it don't get caught on somethin," he said to Méka, or to himself.

She slung her rifle on her shoulder. "I'll miss your playing."

He laughed. "I got a half-decent singin voice if that'll do."

Outside, Greatmother met them where the horses were picketed. Raka's was missing. "You will leave the horses here and take two of our suon," she said. "We're remaining encamped for a while. You can retrieve the horses on your way down the mountain once you've caught the king."

Méka nodded. "We appreciate it. It'll cut our journey in half to have use of the suon."

"It's unfortunate these Kattakans don't allow you to bring your own from the south."

They exchanged looks. Lilley held up his hand. "That ain't my fault."

Méka said, "Do you feel comfortable riding one now?"

"Sure. If they ain't ornery."

"Oh, they're ornery," said Greatmother.

"Take the piebald," Méka said. "She knows you."

The wrangler brought a halter to fit Cottontooth and the suon surprisingly sat patient as Lilley did so. He attached the rein and ran the pack ties over back and belly, cinching his gear securely. Méka chose a cobalt suon gilded around his muzzle and for some minutes offered her hand for him to lick and rubbed the column panel of his neck scales until the gold flare above his brows fanned out in contentment. Lilley promptly named him Dagger and offered his own scent to the cobalt, who sniffed enthusiastically at his shoulder. The air collided with the happy meeting of man and suon.

Soon she and Lilley and a third suon following Dagger launched into the air. Within minutes they hung above the tree canopy with the sunning horizon in the east over a ridgeback of mountains capped by snow. To the west, a darker blue range faded in layers that would lead out to the big waters. She felt the absence below them where Raka remained and formed the image of ground-hugging shrubs and dry soil, eyeing the very location from the air as she rode the suon's shoulders, and cast the impression of it toward the other Ba'Suon. Then she and Lilley winged toward the landing place to wait. Once they'd dismounted, all three of the suon paced a circle some distance from one another and marked the shrubs. Cottontooth squabbled briefly with Dagger and the third suon until they put their faces down with reticent chuffs.

Méka approached Lilley, looking once toward the trees from where they expected Raka to emerge. "There is something we need to talk about before he joins us."

Lilley tilted back his hat. "That sounds ominous."

"I chose to come here to gather the king because I've been experiencing a dream and the rite would afford me a reason both Mazemoor and Kattaka would understand."

His eyes narrowed. "A dream?"

"My people believe that dreams are sometimes the memories of the cosmos, there is no forward or backwards, and as such they can reflect your past or show your future. To the cosmos it is all one flow of time, yet we must discern it. In my dream I was standing on this land. I knew it was this land—the land of my birth—yet it's a land I haven't touched in many years. But I felt a strong connection to it, as to my ancestors and to the suon. So I had to return."

He continued to watch her, listening, and said nothing. Perhaps Sephihalé ele Janan had also spoken of his dreams.

"The land was saturated by the sun. There was a great field and the field was like all the world, without end. I felt the many paths walked by all the Ba'Suon for millennia, our footprints in the golden grass, our dead in the movement of the air. Our suon in the warmth. Such was the vastness."

"Why're you tellin me this now?"

Méka held Lilley's eyes so he couldn't look away. "Because also in the dream there stood a man. I didn't see his face, his back was turned to me, but he stood in the field and there was a deep sense of power to him. Of tumult. Of change. Like a gathering of a storm in the distance. A red shadow seemed to fall around his shoulders. And the more I am in Raka's presence, the more he reminds me of this man in my dream."

Lilley drew a breath, somewhere between a nervous laugh and a look of horror. "Didn't I tell you last night? You gotta be careful with him, and now even your ancestors up in the stars are tryin to warn you."

She shook her head. "That's not what I mean, Lilleysha. I don't know the whole story of what Raka did to you and Janan, but it's devastating what happened to his family. You understand our families are not just our blood relations. It is everyone who's taken the name and walks the same paths under the stars."

Lilley's eyes pinched half-shut. "I know that."

She remembered embracing her own family before she traveled to a Mazoön town to board a ship that would take her through the long waters. Leave-taking always ached and rode the wings of her heart through the absence. She thought of the endless ache that must reside in Raka, for his leave-taking would never lead to reunion. "He must have considered both you and Janan as family. As a Ba'Suon, it's painful to be alone. I'm not justifying anything that he's done but while he's away from Fortune City and Shearoji's command, we can help him. *I* must help him. I believe that's what my dream was telling me. He belongs out here in the land, same as you and me, and the more he feels so, the less likely he'll…repeat what happened in the far north."

Lilley opened his mouth, stared at her for an extra moment, then walked away a couple strides before turning back. His right hand rested on his holster while he rubbed his jaw with the edge of the leather-banded stump. "Look, Méka, I understand that about him. Maybe not like you or Janan, I can't—" He waved his hand to encompass the air, the world. "I don't feel it like you do. But I wanted to help him cause Janan said he was one of us. But he ain't the only one in pain, you know. He showed up in our unit durin the war and Janan welcomed him to our fire when nobody else did. We shed blood together, then that little rat sold us out to Shearoji. I don't trust him and neither should you."

"But why would he do that?" She found it difficult to imagine Abhvihin ele Raka being friends with anyone, much less Lilley at any point. Yet there was a kind of passion to their dislike of each other.

"Cause he didn't want us to leave and he refused to go with us even when we asked." Lilley walked away two steps again and turned his back to her. She watched him take a deep breath. "I reckon he was in love with Janan, even though he'd never admit it. So it was outta spite that he told Shearoji our plans. I made Janan go even if it meant goin without me. It was more important that he got out, for him and his dragon. And now it's been five fuckin years since I've seen him."

The anguish was evident, wavering around him like ripples of a desert mirage.

He spoke to the sky, a flatness to his tone now. "It seems to me Raka kills what he loves. What do you think you can do with that, Méka?"

For a minute the silence suspended in the air with the clarion bell of the sun and the whistle of the trees.

Cottontooth shuffled near, perhaps sensing the distress. *goldcloud arɲd í redsuɲ íɲ fíre* She nudged her muzzle to his shoulder and Lilley raised his hand to stroke it, turning his full attention to her. Méka watched as the turbulence softened around him.

She didn't know what she could do for Raka. She wished she could ask Sephihalé ele Janan. Another Ba'Suon would understand what Lilley, in his own hurt, could not: that fear and suspicion imbalanced the world into chaos, and they couldn't be ignored or controlled by avoidance. That even the ones who betrayed you in love deserved a reckoning with love. But perhaps that itself was a dream when you possessed no family and no love to welcome you back from the long journey of solitude. How did anyone reckon with loss? She stood now on the land that once her family had traversed through all the ages of stone, but back in Mazemoor she had felt the distance, the uprooting of her feet from these paths like a mountain tumbled to the sea from a great quake. No longer anchored to the earth, nor touched by the open palm of the sky.

Now, a slow and subtle anger stirred in the reservoir of memory.

THEY SAT ON the ground and ate some of the fried bread the camp had made them, and drank water from their skins. When the sun disappeared behind a front of blue clouds, Raka walked his bay mare into the shrubland. He held his rifle in the crook of his arm and his gaze marked the new crown of suon. Then he looked at Méka.

"Someone's followed us up the mountain. They're about a quarter day behind."

She stood. "Who is it?"

"Shearoji's guns."

"What the fuck for?" said Lilley. "You're with us already."

"I don't know. But they're armed with dragonshot and they're using that other pit suon to track this one." He looked at Cottontooth.

"You sure you don't know why Shearoji's makin this move?"

Raka looked at him. Looked at Méka. "He probably doubts you'll follow through."

"You saw the posse," she said. The Ba'Suon way.

"Yes."

It was always something with Kattakans. Her documents in Lord Shearoji's hands weren't good enough insurance, so now he sent men. What next, the High Lord of Diam? "We'll deal with them later. That one's for you, Abhvihin." She pointed to the black suon on loan from the Lapliangs. Lilley had already named her Miz Midnight. "We'll get to the Jewel first and get our king."

"Shearoji's king," Raka said.

She kept on watching him. "Are you determined to think so?"

He didn't answer. Lilley said, "You better sort whose side you're on before that posse gets to us."

"Wrangle your suon and shut your mouth," Raka snapped. The heated retort made Lilley laugh, which only seemed to aggravate the Ba'Suon man even more. He unloaded his mount to turn it loose in the direction of the Lapliang camp and dropped the nose of his rifle in Lilley's general direction.

"Let's get on," Méka said, before the Kattakan lost his humor about the situation. She capped her water skin and hissed to Dagger to bring his head up.

In the air, the men on their suon followed her. That Raka was supposed to help her in order to bring the king back to Lord Shearoji was something she wrung in her thoughts until it felt dry and brittle. She looked below at the dwindling stand of dwarf trees and scrabble grass, gravel spreading the higher they ascended the range. By flight they remained ahead of Shearoji's posse.

The air slapped cold against her cheeks and whistled in layers through the hollow scales of their suon. The beat of the wings were unison claps of thunder in their wake. She knew the general locations of the mountain crowns in this region as they had nested there for generations. On foot and horseback, as she'd initially anticipated her journey, it would have taken weeks of sounding the range to pinpoint the exact nests. But it was the suon they rode who knew the precise heights staked by the wild suon. They could smell them, hear them, and sense in that natural way of their kind. An innate territorial awareness and connection to all of nature. A small nudge of inquiry, of intent, was all it took for Dagger to shake his head and bank from their altitude until the target of his flight rose into view like the prow of a great ship.

The cliff's edge spired from the crouching clouds. Speckled on lower ledges of shadowed granite lay the mossy nests of a large crown, the green all ripped from lower elevations and piled with care to form a bed for the cubs. She spied at least five nests spread in jagged intervals down the rock. On each ledge two or three young suon lay curled up, while here and there larger adults flitted back and forth like jeweled bats upon stalactites. Dagger latched himself to a vertical ridge overlooking the gulf between peaks and she wrapped the halter rein around both fists and squeezed her legs around his ribs, glancing briefly at the tops of stunted growth far below. Cottontooth and Miz Midnight clung beside her, their tails carving the air, long necks craning up toward the gray sky.

"Do you see the diamondback?" Lilley called across to her.

"No. This may not be his crown."

"There's a king," said Raka, "but it isn't the diamondback."

A vermilion king soared along the top of the cliff like an arc of spattered blood. Behind him on the rock two bronze-paneled queens reared on their hindquarters and bellowed. The king's wedge-sharp head swung their way, bloodred crest rigid like a shark fin. With both wings flared he gusted a stream of fire in their direction. They were too far to feel even residual heat but it hadn't been meant as a strike.

"He's happy to see us," Lilley said, stroking Cottontooth's neck as she chuffed with agitation.

They flew through the peaks and swept down the mountainside and up again, marking the various nests along this slice of range, focusing mainly on the Jewel. But the diamondback didn't show himself.

"Maybe he migrated," Lilley said once they'd descended to a rock desert to rest the suon.

"No," said Raka. "He was spotted here as recently as last week. He's eating his way through the range like a hurricane and started to battle with some of the other kings."

"And this is the one y'all think you can catch?"

Méka remained aboard Dagger as the men climbed down. "I'm going to scout for Shearoji's posse. Stay here."

She and her suon found the Kattakans with ease, their particular presence full of iron and smoke. They rode muscled horses through the thick columns of soldiering trees and dangerous deadfall, but they didn't hesitate in their ascent up the mountain flank. She didn't have to sight them with her eyes to know they were there. Her suon knew also and blew a kind of cackle into the clouds. Some distance away another suon answered back. A black streak fled across her mind's eye and she knew it was the suon from the pit. She and Dagger remained at a height far beyond the Kattakans' range and soon winged back to the rocky flats upon which Lilley and Raka waited. She half-expected to see the men in argument but they stood each with their own suon and Lilley was laughing with mischief.

"I think I done convinced Raka to shave that rodent off his face."

"What of the posse?" Raka said, ignoring him. But it didn't carry the same irritation as before.

"They're steady on their way."

"I can go warn em off," Lilley said. "My lady wouldn't mind some payback."

"And get her shot?" said Raka.

"Depends on how good their aim is, don't it? I reckon mine's better even from dragonback."

"Now isn't the time to deal with them," she said. "Let them come."

"There's only one way to deal with them," Raka said. "If you want that diamondback."

"For once I agree with him," said Lilley.

She knew it too. But beyond the diamondback there was the matter of returning to her family and answering to the Mazoön government. Neither of which was assured if she crossed Lord Shearoji. Her two companions likely understood that better than she.

They regrouped in the sky. She didn't mark when it happened, but somewhere in their search the tight silence surrounding Raka fell at ease and instead his presence billowed over her like snow, cool and white. Cottontooth, whether by her own accord or Lilley's suggestion, teased Miz Midnight with gentle nudges and the two suon and their riders danced for minutes in the air until Raka dropped his suon down and out the way. It made her smile.

By mid-afternoon they finally identified the diamondback's crown. Six nests perched further up the Jewel peak and far from any other crown. The piebald cloud and the smaller suon labored to climb the heights despite their large lungs, having spent almost a day of winging the thin air with a cargo of people and their supplies. It was Raka who pointed them in the right direction and Méka didn't think it was from his suon's sensing. They'd pulled their hoods forward to block some of the sunrays that lanced between the clouds and when she looked over at Lilley he was drained of all color.

"Drop down," she called to him. "Get your breath."

He didn't debate it. She watched him arrow toward the lower clouds, Cottontooth's gray and white scales blending with the sky's cover. She and Raka idled their suon some miles from the diamondback's crown, the great wings thundering around them and stirring the air like miniature cyclones.

"We need to separate him from the queens and the cubs and drive him to a catch cave. I'll show you where they are." She conjured the impression of them, half a dozen in this region all touched by the Ba'Suon of this land for generations. Perhaps Raka felt their existence regardless. "Once he's in there I'll need you to hold him until I can retrieve Lilley to assist from the lower plateau."

There was a strange challenge in his tone. "What would you have done if it was just you and that Kattakan?"

"I can run the king down myself and Lilley would've been my guard in the lower country. It's just easier with both of you."

From around the edge of his hood she saw his dark eyes glitter. "I shouldn't question one of the kin."

"No, you shouldn't. You know my family name. Can you do this?"

"I won't bring the mountain down around us if that's what you're asking."

"I guess we'll see, brother." She neckreined Dagger around and dropped through the thin atmosphere, the song of his flight like a great roaring wave.

WHEN SHE WAS a child, her father had told her and her brother stories of gathering the king suon of the Crown Mountains with his sisters. A clear mind and a strong song, was what he said. A state of bending perception until the very air coalesced into individual particles in his vision. Until the world winnowed into its unique configurations and he felt every one. Until even with his eyes shut, all of nature, including the great suon, trickled through his mind like rainfall, each part a single drop. He could set his finger against one part and slide it to another, and thus move a mountain. In such a state he could talk to the suon, not in Ba'Suon dialect, but in their language, where their thoughts braided with his own and brought the suon to community.

This was the gift of her family Suonkang.

She circled the diamondback's crown in lazy ellipses and with every circuit felt the air more acute against her skin, then through her skin, her skin itself a sieve through which the world fell. Until the five queens scented Dagger and began to bellow and stand astride the nests so their wings arched over their young. Dagger trembled beneath her from the warning barrage, but she held him with her legs and soothed both sides of his neck with her hands until her suon, like the air, began to sift through the spaces in her insubstantial body. Until nothing but energy and intent seemed to hold them together, but in that holding they were bound and one.

A couple of the adolescent suon hopped onto the narrow cliff face and joined the warning cries with their hoarse trills. A brindle queen launched from one of the nests toward Méka, but Dagger dropped sharply and shot fire to ward her off. Raka rode Miz Midnight from the east, a shadow pasted to the side of the mountain, and as he passed, the crown fell silent. Their bodies bobbed and their wings fluttered, but the noise of them evaporated like rain beneath the hard glare of high noon. For a moment Méka thought the deep resonant hum washing through her was from him, as if the sky itself opened its maw and swallowed them whole. An eclipse of sound. The world thudded shut.

But it wasn't Raka.

As she continued to loop over the crown, a wide

shadow crossed the sun. She looked up and saw a streak of gold and black and white. It blotted her entire vision for a hundred heartbeats as the length of the diamondback coursed overhead like the hull of a war galleon. She reared Dagger as a whip of black tail struck crosswise in her flightpath. The diamondback king made no sound except for the frenzy of wind through his hundred thousand scales, cutting through the fingers of the firmament.

Holding the reins in her left fist, she unlooped the chains from across her chest and back. She gripped tight to Dagger with her legs, locked the two separate chains together and took one end to clap to the center casing that slid back and forth if she gave or released tension to the lead. She grasped the loop and its lead and held it down by her side as the king arrowed back for another pass, his massive body and cloud-spanning wings wholly nimble in his domain of the sky. Her heart pounded until the mountains themselves seemed to echo it back.

The king made no cry, he sent no fire. His yellow eyes faced toward her in his advance, as unblinking and burning as the sun. He saw a small male suon, not the rider, an interloper in his territory to swat away with the least amount of effort. For a shimmering moment as the heavens moved through her, the diamondback's dominant fury coursed like electricity across the shell of her skin. She shook, but she held the looped chain low against Dagger's flank. Because she didn't move, neither did the cobalt, both of them suspended in the air and every particle of it swirling in a slow dance before her as the king suon minutely disturbed the currents around him in his streamlined attack.

At the last moment he flung down his left wing and dove beneath them. His tail sliced up in a long curve to lash them toward the ground, but she had seen it in the flicker of a blink, the hook of a talon, the stand of his crest. Her arm and Dagger's right wing in unison angled down to meet the diamondback's aim, the trajectory led by his head, and she slung out the chain so the circle of it met the larger suon's muzzle. In one move she pulled. It tightened with a snap, and held. The diamondback jerked and reared back his head. She gave the cobalt rein and Dagger rolled and landed, talons latched, onto the black and gold pattern snaking the whale-length of the king's back. She let go of the reins entirely and with both hands heaved on the chain, locking the king's muzzle shut. They began to twist and fall through the air.

Her vision blacked. Her breath stopped and the wind sliced through her like a scythe. She didn't fight it, buffeted by the force of the fall, the world itself an anchor and she the spinning trunk on the tenuous tether of a torn root. Her legs clamped Dagger's flanks. Soon enough the diamondback king balanced himself, spanning his wings fully to soar, jaws straining against the chains. Her eyes opened, struck by blue and gold. When she sounded the world around her, the clouds rang back like cymbals and the sun thudded in hot pulses.

Far below, down the flank of the Crown Mountains and the site of the catch cave deep within ribs of granite, the black and depthless shape of Abhvihin ele Raka swelled up to surround her like a wide and hungry mouth, and in a blink the earth and the cosmos itself fell silent.

FROM ONE BREATH to the next she felt the absence of the open sky. Instead, limestone cave walls arched overhead like broken teeth. She still sat astride Dagger, draped forward along his neck as he trembled and blew, but the chains had disappeared from her grip and she heard them slither and ring a hundred yards deeper in the dark. When she looked around, the golden eyes of the diamondback king stared back. He gave nothing but a sense of never-ending dark in his presence. A shiver rippled through her limbs like the roil of an electric current. Dagger tensed beneath her.

"He's tethered," Raka said, standing at the mouth of the cave. His voice sounded as if from the end of a narrow tunnel. "Lilley's below waiting for us on the barrens."

Her voice was hoarse. "What did you do?"

"I moved you. And the king."

She slid down slowly from Dagger and rubbed his neck until he calmed. Until she could calm. Then she walked unsteadily to the opening of the cave. In the far distance, the Jewel's peak streaked with snow rose toward a dim blue sky. Night descended like a thin dark veil from the stars. She saw no collapse of ancient spine or tumult of the rocky earth below. No new rising flood from interior lakes or overflow from snaking rivers, despite Raka's intercession in the gather, the dregs of which rang and shattered in rolling rhythm in her ears. No, he hadn't brought down the mountain upon their heads even if he characterized himself as all storm. Perhaps that was a fortune to be emphasized, yet it could have also been blind luck.

She looked at his back where he stood in his enfolded absence from the world as if he had never existed and still did not exist even with her wide-awake eyes and all of her Ba'Suon knowing set upon him.

"I know what I'm doing," he said in the hollow voice of a disembodied spirit. "The king knows it too, which is why he won't attack you."

She had never met one of the family Abhvihin before Raka. She understood now the stories from her Greatmother, how they'd been laced with both fear and respect. "You could've warned me."

"No time. The queens were about to strike. It was easier than battling to head them off."

"Easier? More dangerous."

He looked at her. He held nothing in his hands, no weapon or blade, his hat removed, the short tousle of his hair in sweat-damp curls. The dark pinning of his eyes like punched out holes. Shockingly, he had shaved. At some point in her dislocated stupor when she'd lost time and awakened in this cave, he had trapped the diamondback, rested, and shorn that mustache. It seemed to open his expression with a strange guilelessness. His lips twisted in derision at her scrutiny, but all she felt through the residual chime of the world in her ears was his pain. As though a layer had been flayed back, the raw underbelly exposed.

"I've been dangerous this whole ride," he said, "yet you're here. The mountains are still here. Your king is here."

She pressed the palm of her hand to her stomach and looked back at the shifting shadow of the diamondback deep in the belly of the cave. Raka had moved her from one location to the next—not impossible for the Ba'Suon, but in his state of turmoil it was a risk she wasn't certain she would've taken had she known it was his intention. But he never spoke of his intentions.

She looked at him. He was staring out at the vista again. "It's my king now?"

"If you mean to defy Lord Shearoji you'll have to shed blood."

"Blood has only ever led to more blood. It would break the treaty."

He turned to her, a sudden sharp attention. The swollen silence sucked out the natural reverberation of the cave. "It's not *our* treaty. You don't understand how it works here, Suonkang. There is no other way."

"*No other way* are the words of conquerors. Not all resistance is through weapons." She thought of the camps, the rows of wooden structures in which her family and others like them had been filed, fed, and watered at the Kattakans' behest, unable to hunt or commune with the suon. Unable to move through their ancestral paths. Only the stars had seemed free, and reminded them of the freedom they were bound to feel again. She thought of the devastation they'd seen upon release from the camps, the blighted land and suon corpses in mounds of horror. The ultimate result of war. Even through the low running stream of her anger, such memory worked to dampen any sense of vengeance in cold shadow. "You fought in the war, Raka. How could you want that desolation again?"

"Some things require sacrifice. Even Lilley would tell you. His people were slaves to the Kattakans. They enslave their own in some ritual of hierarchy. His family fled the mainland generations ago to be free here amongst the Ba'Suon. Then the Kattakans came here and brought their hierarchy to us. So now we fight alongside them to be free. Blood has been shed already, Méka. It soaks the earth, and the stars have been witness to it before we were born."

This was the most he'd spoken in all the days they'd been together. Like he had finally unshackled some thought and sought to thrust it into her arms. A clearer picture of the reluctant bond between him and the red-haired soldier began to form. All the history of them that she had interrupted and could not now turn her back on, any more than she could her kin.

"Then why have you aligned with Shearoji?"

He spread his hands. "What choice did I have?"

"Be amongst your own people in the mountains. Or

return with me to Mazemoor. The choice you once had with Lilley and Janan."

"And risk killing the southern Ba'Suon like I did my family? The Kattakans remind me every moment that I am outside all kin. It's where I belong. But that doesn't mean I don't want us to be free."

Solitude was against Ba'Suon nature. The static of anger and frustration crackled from his presence so that she felt it like bullets against the cool surface of her skin.

"Janan tried to help you. Why didn't you let him, when you love him so?"

Raka blinked at her. He reared back his shoulders and laughed. The sound of it shocked her. "What?" he said.

"Lilley said you were in love with Sephihalé ele Janan."

He laughed again and looked down into the valley. "Lilley always was a fool."

The entire cave seemed to breathe. It rushed through her ears. "It's not Janan you love."

He didn't reply. Or look at her.

She walked to the back of the cave and met the king. His right foreleg was trapped by a heavy ring of iron installed in the rock long ago by her people. He paced with lumbering steps in the confines of the cave and growled past the clamp of his muzzle, his tail coiling and uncoiling in restless upset. Mirroring the turmoil inside the man who'd brought him here. Only a Ba'Suon connection could keep a king in chains for long enough to warm the bond, but such connection always flowed both ways.

The gnawed carcass of an elk sat in a ragged pile in the corner. *Raka kills what he loves,* Lilley had said. But the diamondback had been soothed enough not to fight, had been fed and remuzzled and now watched her, wary and wanting, but not to kill. Control existed in the man yet he was afraid of himself. Guilt had become his ancestral land.

She returned to the mouth of the cave. Raka hadn't moved but he spoke to her, to the mountains in the distance. "I thank you for trusting me in the gather."

"I didn't have much choice."

"Regardless. A Suonkang of the north country. If your family rallied the other families, we might stand a chance against these Kattakans."

"Is that why you help me? You can barely help yourself. You turned on the men who cared for you—"

"I couldn't let him go." Now he faced her, a confrontational regard. "If I'd let them run from this place, if I'd run with them, it would have been another loss. Once they were free, what care would they have had for me?" His silence pulsed like a heartbeat separate from the chest of its life. Made his words sound empty. "But with you here, maybe there can be some purpose to what the stars have deemed for me. This destruction."

"Your *purpose* isn't to destroy, Raka. The suon are still in your blood, as they are in mine. You brought us safely here. It isn't all destruction." When his stare began to grow opaque she touched his arm, held it through even his instinctive recoil. "I can imagine your people in the white cold and frozen seas. I can imagine the ice suon to which you bonded. I hear they look like clear crystal and the blue of high summer."

"It's so." She saw him remembering. "There's nothing like the sound of the arctic wind through their scales. The suon are pure. That diamondback for all his destruction is also pure."

"Then so are you. You are both children of the cosmos."

He freed his arm from her grip, but only to step further out the mouth of the cave. "There was a glacier suon my family tried to gather. So told our Greatmother. It took four of our family to lower its muzzle, it was so willful. What the Kattakans want out of our connection to the suon is breakage, but it's a covenant. We protect the suon when we're under their wings, as they protect us. This is what they understand."

"I feel it."

"You feel the glimmers. Even a Suonkang who can gather the monarchs of the Crown Mountains must encourage agreement, one that the suon may with inattention break of its own accord. In covenant there is no such consideration. It's a binding oath. Just as there's no such consideration with the rest of nature, for we're covenant with it too."

She finished his thought. "But you broke that covenant when you killed your family."

He wouldn't look at her. The pain shrank to such

a narrow point inside him that its density could have swallowed the world. Could have pulled the world and the stars into the dead center of his chest.

"And you've been punishing yourself ever since. With Lord Shearoji, with Janan. With Lilley and even with the suon in Fortune City, not free and no longer protected, only handled."

"There is no other existence for me. Nature is unforgiving."

"Nature is neutral."

"But it's binding. Break the covenant and it revolts."

He spoke truth but saw it only through the lens of his own sorrow. Any touch to the void inside him rang with repudiation. She walked up to stand by his shoulder and look out.

"It's only a matter of time before the Kattakans get this far into the mountains," he said.

"I know it."

"Down by the Derish they say you used to be able to hear the suon at night, they were so plentiful. They flew over the peaks and even at such distance they sounded like a hurricane."

"Hundreds," she said. "Now they migrate away from settlements if they don't attack outright. My mother told me stories of their flights across the moon, blotting all light for hours. Total night even in the summer months. They would be so spread across the sky that the stars saw nothing else. Now these Kattakans hunt them for sport and food and you don't hear them at all in the valleys."

"Except in the pits. We too used to be plentiful, Méka."

She managed to speak only after a long moment. "It's so."

They stood looking out at the barrens and the trees beyond that reached to the bowl of the heavens like supplicants. He felt to her now like the white tundra on the brink of a storm.

He looked at the diamondback. "Should I talk to him or do you want to?"

"Leave him be for now. We'll chase up a stag for him in the morning. You should come down with us."

"No," Raka said. "I want to sit with him."

Perhaps it was for the best, for both man and suon. A communion without judgment, nature at its most neutral. He unclenched the fist of himself alone with the suon, like she'd felt when he rode Cottontooth. Hopefully they could remain in the backcountry, all three of them and the suon, until such time as he could begin to heal. Away from war and the stink of the city, the plunder for gold. Perhaps he felt the inclination in her now, she let it float freely from the nimbus of herself.

"Lilley did all right," Raka said suddenly. "For a Kattakan with one hand."

"He doesn't hate you, you know. His hurt is born from care." She climbed back astride Dagger and looked down at Raka as he touched the suon's side.

"I know," he said.

"You should tell him you love him."

Raka shook his head, a silent laugh. "You're a needle between my ribs, Suonkang." He slapped the cobalt's hide and in two steps they dropped from the mouth of the cave to the valley below.

LILLEY HAD BUILT a fire in a ring of churned rocks and he knelt before it cooking a rabbit over the flames. Méka unloaded her gear and turned out Dagger to mingle with Cottontooth and Miz Midnight as they nibbled on some yellow draba. Lilley looked up at her as she stood by the fire to warm her hands. The color had returned to his pale features. He pushed back the brim of his hat with his leatherbound stump.

"I flew a circuit for a while. A couple of the queens came down from yonder but we drove em off, me and the lady. She still got some pit fight left in her. Didn't see no other dragons, but I reckon they smell the king and don't want nothin to do with him. I didn't think you'd catch him that quickly."

"It would've taken longer but Raka did something."

"What he do?"

"Something I didn't think he could do without damaging something. Or communicating it to me beforehand. He gave no warning."

"He didn't crash down the moon so I reckon it weren't the worst. Are you all right?"

She found a flat rock close enough to the fire and sat. The ringing in her head had subsided. "I think so. How long until that rabbit's done?"

They ate as the sky deepened. Lilley boiled tea for them and they drank and watched the fire in its hypnotic gambol. Eventually the suon launched into the night to hunt. More than once she caught Lilley looking up toward the cave, which was only a smudge of black in the belly of the mountain. No light or sound emanated from it.

"Is he gonna sleep up there with it?" he said.

"He might."

"You wouldn't find me nowhere near a diamondback king. I don't bet on any irons holdin em."

"You're going to have to stand it as we take him back south."

"You really gonna take it to Shearoji?"

She stared at the fire. "No. To Mazemoor."

"How?"

"I would like to stay longer in the mountains. With you and Raka. He needs it. But I don't know how I can save the king without starting conflict. If we flew the king back to Mazemoor without papers it would be a breach of the treaty. There's no other way but through Fortune City or else both our governments would go through us to get to each other."

Lilley hissed air out from between his teeth. "They ain't my government. I just happened to be in the land same as you and they done organized themselves around me." He rubbed his wrist across his cheek. "As far as Shearoji's concerned you still gotta gather another dragon for yourself, so we got some time before we decide what to do."

"You're free, Lilleysha, you don't have to put yourself in the center of this."

"I reckon I might."

She looked across the flames at him. He sat poking the coals with a stick. They had come up the Crown together, all three of them, and she discovered that she was not yet prepared to leave its heights. For all their battling, she didn't think they wanted to either. She was not a replacement for Sephihalé ele Janan, the third of their unit, but she felt the motions of their attachment were quite similar even to the Suonkang in Mazemoor, and there was comfort in that. There was family in it.

"I wanna go to Mazemoor with you," he said eventually.

"To find Sephihalé ele Janan?"

"Yeah. But I reckon I'm done with Kattaka anyhow."

She nodded. "Did you see Lord Shearoji's posse while you were in the air?"

"I peeked. They're still comin."

"We might have to..." She didn't want to say the words. "If we kill them and let the wild suon have them, we could tell Shearoji we never saw them."

Lilley looked at her straight. "We could."

"If he believes us he might return my papers so we can get back into Mazemoor. You would need documents too."

"Raka would have to back us."

"He will."

"You sure about that?"

"There's only one way to find out. But tomorrow." The food churned unsteady in her stomach and her body ached for sleep. She slung the remnants of her tea into the fire and settled back into the makeshift bedding she'd arranged with her bag and a blanket. She set the rifle at hand and her blades on her other side and she wrapped herself in the wool against the alpine cold. She looked at the orange and blond flames throwing shadows and light in a small pool around them until the warmth grew heavy on her face.

Some time later Lilley said, "Méka."

She opened her eyes and five Kattakan men sat on horseback arrayed on the other side of what was left of the fire. Morning cast a gray sheen over the landscape and their faces. Lilley stood beside her bed and he was holding his rifle. Two of the men braced the stocks of their shotguns against their thighs and another two sat with their hands on their hip holsters. She recognized among them the Mountain Guard from her arrival. The last one, who she gleaned was the leader for how his horse stood ahead of the others, sat with his hands crossed on the pommel of his saddle. They all watched her as she climbed out of her blanket. The leader shook his head once when she reached for her weapons, so she stopped.

"Can we share your fire?" he said.

"There ain't much fire to share," said Lilley.

"I reckon you know how to build one even with one hand."

Lilley didn't move.

"I suggest you go about it, son."

Overhead the black pit suon circled. It had broken down so completely it obeyed these Kattakans. Even from a distance she spied the scars on its body from the pit. When she tried to reach to it with intent it was like touching an open wound. It spat smoke toward her and flung itself higher into the air. Miz Midnight was nowhere. Dagger and Cottontooth stood behind them, wings flexing with tension. Méka took their loose reins and they shifted restless across the rocky ground, crossing in front and behind each other. Cottontooth tossed back her head and bellowed at the sky, the sound of it stark in the cloudy silent morning. Her old enemy bellowed back but didn't descend. The men on horseback shifted.

"You'd best control your dragons," the leader said.

"Why are you here?" she said.

"We been ridin all night and just want a hot meal. Son, you ain't tendin to that fire."

"I ain't much inclined," Lilley said.

One of the men lowered his shotgun toward the suon.

Méka looked at Lilley. "It's all right."

He handed her his rifle and went to the pile of deadfall he'd gathered the night before and began to choose the branches for the fire. The men watched him. They watched her. The leader stepped down from his horse and lifted his hat from off his head. He wiped thick fingers back through his long hair then reset the hat and looked up and around at the valley and the mountains as if seeing them for the first time in the dawn.

"Where that diamondback dragon at?"

"I can take ya for a close-up look," Lilley said, unceremoniously dropping an armful of wood on the burning embers. "I reckon it's his mealtime and you got some girth."

"Nobody asked you, you stumpy bastard. I'm askin the Ba'Suon princess."

"He's in the cave," Méka said.

"Subdued?"

"Take your chances." She watched him look around again until he took note of the mouth of the cave.

"Where's Raka?"

"I don't know."

"We ain't his keeper," Lilley said.

The men got down from their horses. Lilley set his hand on his pistol.

Méka said, "We don't want to fight."

"Good to hear," the leader said. "We come for our dragon. As promised. Lord Shearoji figured it'd be easier to get it down the mountain in pieces."

It was then she noticed the long broad saws strapped to the muscled horses, wrapped in canvas. She felt her fingers press hard into the stock of the rifle. The suon behind her scraped the gravel beneath their talons. The gray of the morning began to strip away in wisps as all but these five men faded to the edges of her knowing.

"You lookin like you're tryin to make a decision," the leader said. "I suggest you don't make a stupid one. There ain't no leavin this country if you make a stupid decision, girl."

She measured the men. "You're not chopping up that king."

"Ain't we now?"

"I'm taking him back to my people, as it says in the treaty between Kattaka and Mazemoor. The Ba'Suon don't hunt suon for you."

"Girl, that fool treaty don't mean shit here in the high country."

The crack of the shotguns startled the suon. When she looked around Cottontooth collapsed to the ground, blood blooming from her ivory forehead, her eyes a fixed muddy yellow. *nothing* where once there'd been life, *nothing* billowing out from the body in shockwaves of absence.

Gunfire split the air around her. Lilley shot one of the men right off his feet. She raised the rifle and fired all in one gesture and the man beside the dead one fell. Dagger launched himself into the sky and screamed fire down at the Kattakans, but they had scattered.

She and Lilley were exposed. "To me," she shouted at the same time she sent *down* to Dagger and he swept low to the ground with wings spread. She caught the halter cheek strap with one hand and stepped onto his foreleg to swing herself behind his shoulders. She felt Lilley land at her back and grasp her waist. The cobalt shot straight toward the clouds with a shove of hind legs into the gravel. The beat of his broad wings forced the Kattakans to stumble.

"Fuckin bastards!" Lilley cried behind her, twisting to look down at where Cottontooth had fallen.

The Kattakans maneuvered to fire on them again but a shadow crossed the sky overhead. A wailing dirge funneled through hollow scales. A sudden bloom of *silence* before]]]] in deafening pulse staggered Dagger in the air and blasted the breath from Méka's lungs. She clung to the cobalt as the diamondback king descended to the churned rocks beside the dead suon, crest tall and fangs bared, his wings arched back and the mass of him shivering the land to the roots of the mountains. Abhvihin ele Raka rode his shoulders.

A surge of wind seemed to racket right through her and separate her skin from her bones. A sound like lava pouring forth from the arteries of the earth rushed through her ears. Her eyes burned. All of it in slow seconds, a stretch of an eternity. She looked below and the Kattakans disappeared into dust, weapons and clothes and the essence of them now particulate matter floating directionless toward the mountains, the sky, the dome of the blind cosmos above as daylight arose like smoke.

The horses bolted, stirrups flapping, reins loose. The diamondback arrowed into the sky. Miz Midnight trailed him. The black pit suon had fled, its fear rippling the ground like an earthquake.

"What the fuck just happened!"

She couldn't answer. Her ears rang. In a single thought she and Dagger and Lilley, clutching the back of her coat, rushed in the wake of the king suon as it headed south toward Fortune City.

WHEN THEY CRESTED the treeline to dip toward the mouth of the Derish River, Fortune City was already burning. Flames whipped as tall as pines. The population ran toward the gold camps and the bay in horrified disarray. Some attempted to escape on the boats or hide in the sawmills. None were spared, not even other Ba'Suon. Only the pay dirt suon fled to the skies, their chains broken. Heat and black smoke blasted in all directions, choking the breath from her throat. Dagger faltered in the flight. Méka brought him down on the sandbar so she and Lilley could dismount. The citizens of the town disappeared all around them in an oil-dark mist like Shearoji's men in the mountains, and at the center of the destruction strode Abhvihin ele Raka.

The absolute silence of it engulfed her, dropping a blindness around all of her senses. She couldn't feel Lilley's presence, even reaching for him. But he caught her hand and that grounded her to the earth. She breathed and eventually heard Dagger blowing with exhaustion and distress behind them. Slowly the world expanded, encompassing a weight from which a heavy sorrow sank. It pinned her feet to the trembling land.

"Raka," Lilley said.

He was walking toward them surrounded by death, the ashes indistinguishable from the cinder and embers tossed from the collapsing buildings and boats. The diamondback king flew in wide circles overhead, bellowing at intervals as though responding to silent questions only he could hear. Strafing fire upon the buildings already burning. Miz Midnight followed like a shadow, a third of the king's size.

Raka's dark eyes looked at Méka. Looked through her. She saw none of him in them, as though in this act of merciless slaughter he had ceased to be Ba'Suon and became instead an indifferent swathe of pure nature. Unreachable as a storm and as vengeful as a man.

"Raka!" Lilley shouted. She saw the other Ba'Suon's gaze shift momentarily to the Kattakan. Torment. Pleading. She squeezed Lilley's hand past the tears and smoke choking them both. "Come back to us," Lilley said, his voice raw. She didn't know whether it was from Lilley or Raka but the image of Cottontooth dead on the barrens filled her vision in a turmoil of pain. The diamondback's shadow swallowed the shore.

From amongst the disintegrating wreckage of Shore Street a tall figure in long coat emerged. Striped beard. Wild eyes. Lord Shearoji in ragged shock but with a rifle in his hands. Raka released Lilley from his stare and turned to the other Kattakan. In unison the king suon bent his long neck, wings like a drum as he hovered over them.

"*No*," she said, as Lilley let go of her hand to draw his gun from its holster.

She held her palms facing Raka and said it again, the word erupting from the hollow in her chest and the electric energy of her spine and the raw red blooding of the tongue inside her mouth. ꓵꝊ ricocheted against the rock of her teeth and the flood of her eyes. The mud beneath her boots began to rise and roll like a tide.

Raka turned to her in the pull of it. And for a fraction of suspended time she thought she felt him reach to her in the depths of the void that cycloned around him, echoing through him, razing bodies from their shells and the elements from the earth. The vast land around her flared gold like the sun had melted itself along the shore. In Raka's eyes that same fire, recognition—then denial. A refusal of her will. Negation of himself, an emptiness like the cosmos without stars. Nothing to witness nor be witnessed.

Something cracked the air like the sound of a glacier calving. Smoke suspended from the end of Lilley's gun and she saw Lord Shearoji's arm snap back. The rifle jerked upward and its bullet shot toward the clouds in echo.

Something else seemed to exhale behind her right ear. The breath of release. Of succumbing. And Abhvihin ele Raka, her brother in the families, fragmented into such tiny points of salt and light that for a moment even with her eyes closed the last image of him formed like a constellation in her mind.

She felt his death slice through her, deeper than his living silence. A cry burst jagged from her throat.

The dirge of the diamondback roared overhead. ꛯ ꓵꓭ ꝪꞇꝊꝌꙅꓵꓭ ꓰꝪꞇꝪꞇ ꓰꓵꝊ ꛯ

She opened her eyes and looked for Lilley. He stood

with his back to her, the land and water a single swathe of gold, flames from the suon fire setting the world ablaze. A haze of red floated around his shoulders as though the air itself sweated blood.

Then he was collapsing to the ground and the king suon suddenly swept low and caught him in his great jaws. The diamondback ascended with the sound of thunder and storm straight into the ash white sky, and on toward the blinding round mouth of the sun.

DAGGER KNEW TO take her to the Lapliang camp in the mountains. To return home. Somewhere in the sky, Miz Midnight caught up and carried with them. Méka held to the neck of her mount and wept into the cool panel of iridescent scales, but the wind stole even her tears. When they landed in the center of the camp, Greatmother and the others reached for her. Greatmother gathered her into her arms but such cold blew through her that she couldn't stop shivering. Before they reached the door of the big mata, all of the world caved in on itself, into the dark.

She awoke to warmth and layers of woven blankets piled on top of her. Her boots removed. The sound of suon and goats somewhere outside, distant voices. Children playing. A chorus of familiarity but she felt absent from herself. She lay in an empty mata save for Greatmother sitting beside her on the bed.

"Lilley." She pressed the heels of her hands to her eyes. "Raka. All those people."

Greatmother placed a hand on Méka's forehead. "Lilley is in another mata. Rest, daughter."

Perhaps it was only suggestion, perhaps it was more. Either way she couldn't fight it, so she didn't. When she awakened again, Greatmother was squatting by the stove boiling water for tea. The world felt a little less distant but her whole body labored to move, limbs heavy, muscles stiff. She sat up and leaned her elbows on her knees. She could not recall what had been dream and what had been real. Maybe there was hardly a difference.

"The diamondback brought Lilley here," Greatmother said.

Méka looked up.

"It's waiting for him further up the mountain. Keeping watch."

With what clear thought she could muster, she tried to remember, but a part of her shied from it. Raka moving through the city laying waste to all. Shouts of terror cut off like the slamming of a door on an argument.

Lilley's voice, *Come back to us.*

Greatmother came to her with a cup of tea and pressed it into her hands. But she was already trying to escape the blankets and the bed. "I need to see him."

"Not yet. Drink this tea."

"Greatmother—"

"Not yet, daughter. Lilley's asleep anyway. He hasn't yet woken up."

"Did you see what happened?" The way Ba'Suon saw.

Greatmother urged her again to drink the tea. So she did. It was bitter and dark but it steadied her nerves. Filled her mouth with something other than iron and ash.

"I saw enough," said Greatmother. "And I'm afraid our red and gold Kattakan will never be the same." The matriarch eased herself to the foot of the bed and as Méka continued to watch her, she drew a breath and looked across at the door of the mata. "Raka gave himself to Lilleysha."

"What do you mean?"

"Abhvihin ele Raka exists in Lilley. And the king suon. They're bound."

"I don't understand."

Greatmother took the teacup from her hands. "Go to the mata. You'll know which one. See for yourself."

On her feet and outside, the world seemed strangely ordinary. Dagger chuffed at her in greeting but otherwise seemed unaffected by recent events. Children were feeding the goats and fowl. A young man tended the outdoor firepit, a rack of fresh fish waiting to be salted and cooked. A wrangler rubbed down Miz Midnight with a rough cloth and she looked at Méka in recognition when she passed. It was the woman who'd given Lilley the necklace. She looked away as though the sight of Méka saddened her.

Méka followed a certain heaviness in the air through the camp until she stopped at one of the smaller mata on the edge of the clearing. Inside, Lilley lay on one of the three beds closest to a low burning stove, naked shoulders showing from beneath a pile of bear fur. He still wore the red and gold necklace. He had a tattoo on the curve of his right shoulder, a Ba'Suon pattern of circles and stars to represent the cosmos. Existence. Within the pattern was a darker mandala like an abstract entwining of two hands. *Belonging to all, beloved of one.* Her parents had such tattoos. Only a Ba'Suon kusha would know to ink those lines for bonding and she wondered if Sephihalé ele Janan possessed its twin. So many things she didn't know about this Kattakan and yet she felt like she had somehow failed him as she watched him lying there in a false sleep. His eyes were shut and only one lamp hung lit on the wall above his head, casting shadows across the painted interior canvas of the mata. Elk dancing. Suon in flight. Like a diorama turning around him or some manifestation of his dreaming state.

She sat on the edge of the bed and touched his shoulder. His breaths were steady but shallow. All Ba'Suon became used to the presence of Kattakans, their particular dullness. Their lack of conscious connection in the breadth of the cosmos. This Kattakan was different with his muted *goldshard*—yet beneath that moved something darker now, and the longer she held her palm on his bare shoulder, over the tattoos, the stronger she felt it. A subtle current like what suspended in the air before a storm. The depth of something looming. The threat of engulfing.

She pulled her hand away. "How is this possible?"

"I don't know," Greatmother said from the doorway.

"Nobody in the family has ever heard of such a thing. Possibly nobody in any of the families, except perhaps the family of the far north. But we can't ask them."

"Is he ever going to wake up?"

"I think the diamondback waits for it."

She looked up at the shadowed images on the wall of the mata, pressing a hand against the bristled hair of her skull where her tattoos, like Lilley's, reflected the cosmos and her lineage among the stars.

"He was in my dream," she said. Greatmother watched her, silent. Méka met the matriarch's knowing eyes. "I dreamed before I left Mazemoor. About our land. And a man. I'd thought the man was Raka. That I needed to be here to meet him. But then I saw Lilley amidst the flames, shrouded in red. That red was Raka. It was both of them all along. But why does Lilley feel like no other Kattakan? Is it because of his connection to Sephihalé ele Janan? To Raka even before this?"

Greatmother sat by her side. "All people, even Kattakans, are a part of the world and the cosmos. They've just forgotten." She touched Lilley's shoulder and urged Méka to do so again. "But some part of him remembers. As do you."

Two weeks later, Lord Shearoji on horseback entered the camp. It was morning and the wranglers, with whom Méka had aligned herself, had just returned from an elk hunt. Méka's hands and forearms were bloody from the kill and breaking down the animal in the hills. Her blades, which she'd retrieved from her and Lilley's last encampment, swung at her hips. Behind her one of the young men hauled the sledge on which they'd laid the elk and bound up its internal organs in separate skinbags.

The Kattakan lord seemed cautious at this scene. He was alone, and he wore the regalia of the Fortress, the double-breasted black wool jacket tailored to his big lean form, jade red buttons and the red tiger emblazoned on his chest. He carried a rifle, though he kept it in its saddle scabbard and did not dismount. He told the camp that the High Lord Oura Ban requested Méka appear before her Fortress court in the island's southland.

It had been just a matter of time before the news of the slaughter at Fortune City reached the Fortress and some accounting, even a reckoning, of the incident would be called upon. The Kattakans needed someone to blame for the destruction of the gold city. Méka still didn't have her papers to cross the border back to Mazemoor and she wouldn't leave without Lilley anyway. She'd expected this, and the High Lord expected compliance, sending only a single soldier for the task. Or perhaps it was arrogance. The Fortress knew exactly where the Lapliangs were encamped because it was a part of their permission to exist on the land. As Ba'Suon they must always account for themselves.

"I'll gather my gear," Méka said as she washed her

arms at a barrel filled with rainwater. The whole camp fell silent. When she looked up, Lilley had appeared on the edge of the small crowd that had formed. They moved aside for him.

He was pale and thin from two weeks lying abed, asleep and barely nourished. She had sat by him, squeezing drops of water into his mouth from a warm cloth. Somehow he maintained his breath and some strength. His hair blew in the mountain breeze like flames. He held the bear fur around himself but still shivered, and his eyes looked gray in the overcast light.

"I'm comin with you," he said. If Lord Shearoji thought to protest, the idea quickly died when the diamondback suon swept over the camp. The king cast a thick shadow and a swathe of silence, stirring the smaller suon into nervous stamping and staccato calls. The lord's horse reared and cried and he struggled to calm it. Lilley stood motionless, watching. Méka went to him with her red-stained hands and he only moved his gaze from Shearoji and the agitated mount when Méka was standing directly in front of him. His fingers were white, holding the fur tight around himself. "Somethin's happened," he said.

"I know."

"I can hear that dragon." His gaze tilted up toward the diamondback. "He wants to go."

"We can't fly to the Fortress. If we tried it would only make things worse."

He nodded. "First, I gotta siddown."

In the big mata he asked after Cottontooth. She told

him that she and the Lapliangs had returned to the barrens and burned the body under witness of the stars, and honored the smoke that had risen. She told him that Cottontooth was at rest among her ancestors in the mountains and would one day be born anew in another suon and perhaps that one, should they ever meet, would recognize him and the kindness he had shown her. He wept for the piebald cloud and his stare slid away from her face and looked toward the stove, which sat fireless and black.

She touched the leather gauntlet wrapped around his stump. "I've tried to know the diamondback suon but he is also..." She thought of the precise words. "It all just scatters when I try to touch him. Do you understand? Yet you can hear him." She didn't let go of him. She didn't know if he had taken in her words because he said nothing for what seemed too long. The life outside the mata sounded muted, like people speaking in murmurs.

Eventually Lilley said, "He wants to move," and that was all.

GREATMOTHER SENT THEM off with satchels of food and water. She kissed their heads, holding their faces in her strong gnarled hands that had wrangled many suon in her day. That could still wrangle a king. The rest of the Lapliang family bid them off with raised hands. They rode the horses Lord Shearoji had loaned them all those days ago and led the bay mare, the one that had been Raka's. Méka tied the reins to her pommel, and with the Kattakan lord leading they made their way back down the mountain. The king suon followed them from above and unnerved Shearoji and his horse the entire way. He seemed somewhat chastened and asked early on why the dragon harried them. Méka said, "You told me to gather him, didn't you? If you still desire to chop him up for food you are welcome to try." It put that line of questioning to rest.

"What's the matter with him?" Shearoji nodded to Lilley, who remained silent all this time.

But something in the question seemed to provoke him. "I lost my hand in your fuckin war, you threatened Janan and his dragon til he had to run away, you bullied this Ba'Suon woman up the mountain and Raka's *dead*. You need another reason, you piece'a shit?"

The diamondback bellowed from high in the clouds. Lord Shearoji darted a look. When nothing descended upon their heads he snarled at Lilley. "You shot at me to save his life. The deaths of those people are on *you*."

"The hell they are."

"Is that what your High Lord thinks?" Méka said, drawing the men's attention away from each other. Lilley rode with his hand on his pistol.

"You'll hear what the High Lord thinks soon enough," Shearoji said.

At night the man slept, supposing they would have no place to run off to, or would be caught if they did. Or perhaps he'd taken the tenor of their intentions and knew they'd agreed to this journey. There was no other way back into Mazemoor but through the Kattakans and their business.

Méka sat near Lilley and watched the stars emerge from the sky, the great paths of knowing that led into eternity. The moon reclined like a woman between the distant peaks. Lilley grew stronger with each meal and the diamondback remained close enough they heard him breathing wherever he landed. The faint metallic aroma of his piss drifted over the small camp. Lilley didn't seem frightened by it, but a certain numbness imbued all of his gestures, like he was moving through water or fog. He drew on his cigarette with slow inhalations, as if he expected the smoke to twist into something else.

"I don't understand why he did what he did."

She'd chewed on this very thought until it became stale in her mouth. "Maybe we never will. I don't think he was in the world like we are. But he loved you."

Lilley laughed around the cigarette, the sound of raked coals. "Somehow I knew that."

"He was afraid to lose you if he went south with you and Janan."

"The maddening thing is we coulda loved him back maybe, the both of us. But he couldn't accept the prospect of that in the end. The selfish bastard."

She didn't know what to say. They watched the fire together. Behind them, the forest; ahead, the charred remains of the city on the marsh. The desiccated winch towers, collapsed sawmills. Blackened gravel like the volcanic leavings of a molten inferno. When the wind howled it could have been the voices of the dead but she sensed no life, not even remnants.

"I feel like somethin's movin in my chest," he said. "All the time. Like that king dragon's got me on a leash."

"It might be the only reason you're awake and speaking."

"The dragon?"

She touched his wrist. "Yes. He made a covenant with the king to ride him. Now he's yours."

"The diamondback?"

"Raka too. I think maybe there's no difference now."

Lilley flicked his cigarette into the flames. "That son of a gun had to hurt me to keep me, didn't he?"

THEY AWOKE TO gunshots. She stood up out of her blanket holding her rifle. Lord Shearoji was firing into the air as the king suon made off with his horse— saddle and all—locked in the iron jaws. The man swore and kept firing long after the bullets would've had any effect. The diamondback disappeared into the clouds. The lord turned to them and swore hot into their faces. Méka watched without expression as Lilley burst into laughter.

"Guess your horseflesh was easier'n runnin down an elk or a bear."

Méka spoke before Shearoji turned that gun on them. "I'm sorry for your mount. We have the third you gave us." She motioned Lilley to his feet. "The horse didn't deserve that."

"I know it, but maybe he oughtta be grateful he weren't on it at the time."

After coming out of his numb state, Lilley seemed to possess little control over his reactions. On the last few miles to the river mouth he sang a lilting tune he said came from his childhood. He'd never talked about his childhood. She tried to ask him about his family but he drifted away from the question and spoke no more.

They followed the Derish River until it emptied into the sea. Anchored far off-shore sat a Fortress whaling ship, its towering masts with their wrapped sails knitting the clouds into a single hoary mass. They waited on the sandy banks as a wide scow steamed toward them and the diamondback circled the water and the shore in wide arcs. The handful of sailors manning the scow glanced up nervously, but Méka and the men coaxed the horses aboard and soon scuttled back to the ship. Once she and Lilley climbed on deck with their gear, the diamondback began to wing high over the ship's crimson flag of Kattaka, its white underbelly blending with the sky. The captain in her gold collared frock coat stood on the deck and looked up at the suon then looked at Méka. But it was Lilley who said, "Don't try to bring him down with your cannons and you'll live."

Lord Shearoji left them without a word. They were stowed in the same cabin below decks and told not to leave it except for the toilet. Food would be brought. Méka wondered if the suon would tear the ship apart to set eyes on him, but Lilley shook his head. "He knows we're in here. You won't let what happened to Raka happen to me, will you?"

He lay on the lower of the two bunks. She sat at a narrow writing desk and looked at this wooden space with its small round window lined in brass and told herself she could last this burial for however long it took. "You won't end like Raka."

"How do you know?"

"He was afraid to let anyone help him. But we'll go to Mazemoor when this is all over. We'll find Janan and I'll teach you to know the way the Ba'Suon know."

"But I'm not Ba'Suon."

She pulled at her own fingers. She couldn't tell him that she didn't know if she could help him. Greatmother hadn't known. Her family might equally be at a loss. But such truths wouldn't benefit anyone in the present. "You won't end like Raka."

He didn't speak for a long moment. "Have you ever been inside a ship?"

She shook her head. "Coming here I slept up top on the barge. And on the deck of the whaling ship. When we left this island long ago we slept up top even in the rain."

"You'll be all right." He reached across to her and clasped his hand over both of hers. The pressure felt welcome and he seemed to know it. He tightened his grip. "You ever hear about the seventy-year-old horse?"

She laughed in relief. He laughed too and she remembered dancing with him in the mata, drunk on honey liquor. His smile with its strange baby fangs.

He still smelled like horse and rain. Like the clean earth and sky.

She said, "When we go before the High Lord, let me speak. Let them assume the suon is mine. They won't understand what's been done to you and if they find it curious they might never let you leave."

He nodded and didn't let go of her hands. She moved from the desk to the edge of his bunk, ducking her head so it wouldn't knock the bed above. The ship rocked around them but she found some steadiness looking into his eyes. Maybe she attempted to see something of Raka in the smoky blue, but there was nothing on the surface, only in the pulse when she reached toward the elements beneath skin and bone. The flow in blood vessels, the emptiness of air between the very color of his blood like pathways of venting deep within the world's core. If she followed that stream she would never see the sun again.

SHE COULDN'T FULLY sleep in the tight enclosure so lay staring at the bit of moonlight that shot through the porthole like a roving eye. Other nights there was no light but the summer dusk at this latitude, so she listened to the snap and gulp of the vessel as it parted the waves. She thought of her family in Mazemoor, how they were waiting and didn't know what had happened on her journey back to their ancestral land.

Lilley awoke in the nights. He said he dreamed of the ice suon of the far north, that in his dream the snow blinded him. Sometimes he didn't realize he was awake and asked her if being in the belly of this ship was a dream. If they were actually somehow in the belly of a dragon and the creak of the ship's great frame was in fact the bending of bones as the dragon winged through the sky. She reassured him that they were on their way to the Fortress in the southland, though she gave no guarantees as to what they might encounter once they were there.

After four days and nights on the water the whaler brought them to the port of Diam. She had never been to the big Kattakan cities of the south and in the fell hour the shore and the hillsides winked and glowed even more brightly than the stars overhead. She and Lilley stood on deck and he smoked and flicked the ashes into the dark waters. The cool briny air from the sea dampened into a thicker scent of decay by the docks. Fortune City in its glory seemed now a child's copy, a rough outline of the capacity for occupation these Kattakans possessed. Warehouses and dark fish markets and smaller buildings with signs unreadable in the shadows lined the docks. She heard dogs barking.

"Home," Lilley said, but without any hint of warmth in his tone. "My parents were slaves to a wealthy family in this city."

She remembered Raka's words. "And you? Before the war?"

He looked at her and dropped his cigarette into the water. "I earned my freedom from the war. But it didn't last."

Lord Shearoji and the ship crew unloaded the horses down the dock ramp. They left the whaler behind as they mounted and followed the Kattakan lord along the pier street in an ascent to the Fortress. In silhouette from below, the triangular tiled roofs with their upswept edges and spires seemed to carve into the cloud-streaked cosmos, intricate cutouts that spoke of centuries of artistry and dominance. The walled Fortress sprang from a hill overlooking the winding segments of the city, hung with the red banners of the ashregarat of this land—the military ruling class on display through the spiked circlet of bristling cannons pointed at the sky in backdrop. On every street an array of black and white lanterns illuminated trees dripping with green leaves and summer blossoms of vibrant color muted in the night. Few people walked the narrow stone roads, but their passing on horseback garnered stares from faces half-hidden beneath wide-brimmed hats. Men and women in high-belted robes of geometric and nature patterns, soft-soled shoes, trim jackets, and long flowing vests. Even in the dim light the fabrics spoke of wealth and means.

She and Lilley in their bedraggled wool and furs, the soft chime of suon scales, their sheathed weapons were a subtle disturbance to the veneer of civil occupancy. She could barely comprehend the size of Diam. She felt swallowed by the snaking alleys disappearing into hollows, the endless plateau of tiled roofs like waves of the ocean when she looked behind them on the climb up the hill. The diamondback had disappeared toward the dawn light on the upper reaches of the mountain. Lord Shearoji visibly relaxed. They were met at the iron gates of the Fortress by two standing guards in similar black and crimson, though these held long guns that glimmered in the yellow lantern light. They passed through into a wide empty courtyard of patterned granite and border trees blue in the deep night, their white blossoms like holes punched through the shadows to emit dapples of glow. Lord Shearoji disappeared into the dark when a short man in layers of green and ivory robes approached from an inner chamber. He waited as they dismounted.

"Welcome on behalf of the High Lord Oura Ban. Come with me, Lady Ba'Suon." His eyes, pale behind thin wire frames and round glass, looked Lilley up and down.

"I'm with her," Lilley said.

The man's hands were hidden inside his long sleeves. After a brief moment of thought he nodded and turned to lead them further through the courtyard. "You will rest tonight," he said over his shoulder. "Wash yourselves. Eat. The High Lord will see you tomorrow precisely at noon."

"Precisely," Lilley echoed, looking at Méka. She watched the shadows. Some of them materialized in passing as more guards standing like obsidian columns along their path. The warrens of the Fortress were all hewn polished wood with red undertones, as though bathed in blood. Engraved paneled glass led to hidden rooms, with images of suon and tigers and warriors with long blades and fanned robes. The white shards reflected the lantern lights hung along the way in measured intervals. The High Lord's servant showed them into a room appointed with a wide flat bed and hanging rose silks with scenes of mountains and snake-limbed trees weeping feathery leaves. A long window like the frame of a painting stood open and the summer breeze stirred the silks. Beyond it the silhouette of more trees.

The servant inclined his chin a couple times and cleared his throat. "We did not anticipate your companion. Should he prefer a separate room, I will see to its arrangement."

"It's fine." She didn't trust either of them to be alone in this place where they couldn't get to each other if needed.

The High Lord's servant looked at their faces, then at their weapons and road-abused attire, bowed his chin again and backed from the room, pulling in the double doors with a brisk flair of his sleeves.

She walked the perimeter. A sliding screen led to a place for washing, all of it solid sheets of dark finely grained wood, green glass, and polished speckled stone. Even there they had lit a fire on a bed of coals and the smoke rose up through iron piping, the remnants of its scent permeating the space along with the flower petals sitting in porcelain bowls all around the bath. In the bedchamber another fire leaped and played with the shadows ensconced in the wall. Lilley had dropped his gear and weapons in a corner and sat on the edge of the bed to pull off his boots.

After their separate baths they dressed in the night linens laid out for them on a low chaise and lay side by side on the bed. It was so spacious their shoulders didn't even touch. She heard nothing, not even nocturnal birds or insects. It was as if this Fortress had swallowed them from the world.

"Look." Lilley pointed.

Suon masks reminiscent of what had hung in the fighting pits of Fortune City stared down at them from the opposite wall. It took some time for her to realize they were not masks, but severed heads somehow frozen in expressions of life. The bared fangs and flared nostrils. The angled gold eyes and arching brows. She felt Lilley come to the same conclusion and they both rolled to their sides so as not to look at the heads, but at each other instead. She hadn't seen his face clean in some time. The bridge of his nose scattered with faint freckles. He seemed another man entirely, and when his eyes shut and his breathing steadied, the boyish part of him settled in his countenance. Gently, she laid her hand on his chest.

In the morning they were brought meals of rice and thinly sliced pork and pickled vegetables and tea. The High Lord's servant also brought them clothes and directed them to wear them as these Diam Kattakans. Belted robes over silk-lined trousers and soft cotton shirts with stitched collars of gold thread. All in shades of dove gray and pale reds, as some uniform of servitude. They washed their faces and Lilley dressed as given, but Méka wore again her wool coat and furs.

She polished the dappled gray suon scales on her coat until the light glinted off them, then the suon bone of her blades which she wore at her hips in the manner of her people. Lilley looked at her and smiled. When the servant returned for them he said not a word, but his eyes behind his spectacles squinted and his mouth formed a thin line as if to reinforce some invisible border that should not be crossed.

The court of the High Lord Oura Ban required climbing half a hundred wide steps framed by red engraved columns and those obsidian guards. Overhead the blue noon sky shone through an intricate domed ironwork, as though all petitioners to the court were ascending to some suon-sized aviary. Red and gold banners hung from ceiling spikes and stirred gently in the breeze that furrowed through the court and skated along polished quartz floors lined with the same bloodred wood. Her and Lilley's footfalls echoed across the expanse and, even when they stopped, went ahead of them up to a broad dais where two red jade tigers flanked a red throne inlaid with gold and opal. They were not alone in the court, but watched by dozens of people in dress much like Lilley's new attire, but with far more decoration in braids of gold chains and pearls and jewels so that any small movement brought a musical reminder of the affluence at every turn.

Seated on the dais with her arms spread on her throne, the High Lord watched them approach with a painted gold face of impassivity. Her robes waterfalled around her in several carefully enfolded layers of gold, crimson, black, white, and emerald green. Her dark hair twisted above her head like the horns of a majestic beast, its bulbs entwined with gold and rubies. Her mouth a glossy streak of black paint like the coals from which diamonds were born. So much gold in this city, and for the first time Méka understood where all the toil in the northern fields had gone.

Lilley bowed before this woman. Méka did not.

The bespeckled servant stood at the level of the High Lord's feet and announced to the court, "The High Lord Oura Ban welcomes Ba'Suon Mékahalé Suonkang."

"Why does she not bow?" said Oura Ban.

The court's silence seemed to deepen in the wake of the question. Lilley stood just behind Méka's right shoulder, but she felt how he didn't look at her and she didn't look at him.

"You aren't my lord," she said.

The gold-painted face showed no expression. "I had heard your people were impertinent but now I see the proof."

Méka watched her with a hand resting on the hilt of one of her blades. Her fingers tightened around it.

"Are those the storied blades of the Ba'Suon dragoneers?"

"It's so."

"I should like to see them up close. Lord Shearoji, bring them to me."

From the edges of the courtiers strode the tall figure of the Kattakan lord, in dress much like Lilley, sashed with a streak of red silk. His metallic gray eyes were angry. Méka felt his rage at her apparent impudence bulging toward her like the cloud of an explosion. He held out his hand and flicked his fingers.

"No," she said.

The court murmured behind her.

"No?" said Oura Ban.

"Only the wielder of these blades may touch them."

"And why is that?"

"Because you have to earn them."

Something close to a smile briefly creased the gold façade of the High Lord's face. "How do you earn them, Ba'Suon?"

"You gather a suon."

"Well." The High Lord raised her right hand and waved it in a circle. "All of Kattaka knows that I have taken the heads of dragons in my military exploits."

"Yes, after you've bombarded an adolescent with a dozen cannons. To gather a suon isn't to kill it."

Lord Shearoji stepped toward her.

"No, no," said Oura Ban in a tone of mockery. "This girl is bold and we must admire it. She has captured a diamondback dragon and she has brought it to Diam. To do with Diam what she has done to Fortune City."

"I wasn't responsible for Fortune City and neither was the suon."

"No? So it's Lord Shearoji's imagination, and the imagination of those few survivors, that a king dragon razed the city with its fire?"

"The suon was cajoled to it by Raka, one of Lord

Shearoji's men. Raka is now dead, so if you seek someone to blame, blame the man who set Raka on my rite. I was given permission to gather a suon from the Crown Mountains, as my people have done for generations. If I had been left to it, I would be back in Mazemoor already with the suon—and Fortune City would still be standing."

Murmurs arose from the court. Lord Shearoji's arms folded inside his robes. The iron dome above them almost seemed to ring.

The High Lord's voice lifted above it all, and created silence. "How does one cajole a dragon, Ba'Suon?"

"You speak to it." Méka looked at Shearoji, at the servant at the feet of the High Lord's throne. At the High Lord.

"How do you speak to a dragon, Ba'Suon?"

"To understand that you would have to be one of the family."

"Give me your blades, Ba'Suon."

"No."

Lilley shifted his weight beside her. He was weaponless but pulsing *bloodred*. Somewhere from the heights, the beat of a suon's wings echoed like a rhythmic drumming.

"You bring a dragon to my Fortress," said the High Lord, her voice arching upward like the blare of a battle horn. "You dare even more to refuse the ashregara of Eastern Kattaka."

"I refuse the High Lord what she has no right to, and the suon followed of his own free will when you summoned me here. If you don't allow my companion and I to leave this country, I bear no responsibility for the suon's actions."

The court erupted with voices. The High Lord made a signal with her hand to her servant and the man looked out over the court and dismissed them all in a strong and resonant tone. Méka and Lilley stood on the grand quartz floor as the people filed out behind them. Lord Shearoji watched them, and the High Lord watched them, and the servant in his voluminous robes tucked his hands back into his sleeves and made his shoulders small. The obsidian guards did not leave.

"You speak of cajoling dragons yet somehow you refuse to cajole this king dragon to leave my city."

"There are never any guarantees with the suon. They obey at their own will."

"I could have you shot," said the High Lord.

Méka looked at her unblinking. The drumbeat of the suon wings grew closer. Others began to gather beneath it, making kinetic patterns through the tall air of the court. Shaking the lacquer of the columns. The howl of the wind through the scales of the approaching suon seemed to wind up to a higher pitch. "We require papers to re-enter Mazemoor. Lord Shearoji had confiscated mine, and my permit, before the city burned."

"Is that a threat?"

"I am suggesting to her High Lord what is required for the king suon to leave her city."

She heard the High Lord inhale but her chest did

not move from beneath the layers of silks. The dark eyes flickered up to the sky, to the beat of wings and the shriek through hollow scales, now like a torrent of approaching thunder. The High Lord looked at Lilley as if to refocus her resolve.

"What is your name, Kattakan?"

"Havinger Lilley, milord."

"And what is your relationship with this Ba'Suon?"

"Well, milord, she bought me out. Along with a pit dragon, fair and square. Three pure gold bars if I remember right. I reckon I might not've been worth it as Lord Shearoji took exception to her actions and now here we all are."

"You are a slave."

He lifted his leatherbound stump. "I was a soldier in your army, milord, and it weren't no damn different. But now I'm a free man."

His voice fell into an echo in the almost empty room. The High Lord regarded them for some time in her motionless pose. A wind had started to streak above the dome of the court and carried the sound of trees toward them. The cries of raptors hunting game. And now the rapid pulse of suon wings enveloped the mountain on which sat this fortress, cutting through the gentle ripples of nature. And with the marshaling of a suon storm came the bellow of the diamondback king almost overhead. Countless suon roared back in response. Faintly, screams of the citizenry below in the city floated up to the court. The hollow grind of the cannons maneuvering into position.

"High Lord," said Lord Shearoji, with some urgency.

The servant of the High Lord cowered and flinched, and Shearoji himself cast his gaze upward with a stiffening of his shoulders. But Méka and Lilley did not move or look away from the woman on the throne. Perhaps she would risk a battle between the diamondback, the crown he had rallied, and her cannons. The suon roared again, a fugue of wild voices, sounding closer.

All the gold of the High Lord's visage began to shine with perspiration. "Draw up their papers," she commanded. Her fingers gripped the edges of her red throne. "And get these barbarians out of my country."

LORD SHEAROJI ESCORTED them from Diam to the southern white cliffs of Kattaka. His gaze remained pinned to the sky as the king suon followed them from the air, winging low sometimes to chase birds for play, then arrowing up toward the sun and a drift of thin clouds collecting toward the sea. As soon as the High Lord had ordered their release, the mountain crown cajoled by the king had dispersed while the diamondback sent *I AND REDSUN I AND SKY* through the roof of the earth. And Lilley had looked at her and smiled.

It took some hours of steady riding and none of them spoke for most of it. Lilley seemed to sink into his own thoughts, chin to his chest, and Méka watched Lord Shearoji as the man held his adamant silence. The anger had simmered and a subtle shade of something close to shame seemed to flash beneath it.

The lush green ground felt soft beneath the horse's hooves and when they stopped to water themselves the animals were happy to crop the grass, tails flicking, unbothered even by the suon. The king tended to settle somewhere close and piss his mark before taking off again into the sky. In the distance a strip of gray sea shimmered in the late daylight. Méka stroked her horse's mane and looked at Shearoji over the saddle.

"You truly had no idea what Raka was capable of, did you?"

Lilley looked up from where he sat on the grass facing the water. Lord Shearoji didn't look at either of them, but stood with his hand on the grip of his holstered gun and squinted toward their backtrail.

"He had seemed more Kattakan than Bastard," Lord Shearoji said.

"Even in the war?" she asked.

"In the war he did as he was ordered and nothing more." Now the iron eyes turned to her. "Are you all capable of such destruction?"

She considered what the truth would mean for this Kattakan and for her people who were already regarded as threats that should be tamed.

"Raka wasn't common," she said.

"That's not what I asked, Bastard."

Lilley climbed to his feet. Méka rested her arms up across the back of the saddle. "My people decided to live with your people rather than wage a war that would destroy this land and those within it. But there might be more who thought as Raka thought—that the time for acquiescence is over. It's a much better course of action to be in balance, Lord Shearoji. To not live as slaves or servants or at the whim of a persistent force. That is what I think."

When they came to the edge of the cliffs Lord Shearoji reclaimed the horses and left them. In the glinting blaze of a setting sun they could just discern the hazy northern front of Mazemoor across the molten colored waters raging far below. The diamondback suon circled once more before he alighted on the green and arched back to fan his gold-patterned wings in praise to the open sky. The pink sunlight bore through the skin and scattered the beams in all directions. Méka watched as Lilley approached the king and held out his hand until the suon lowered enough for the man to stroke the white panel of scales along his neck. They stood like this for some time and no words were said aloud, only the low staccato rumble of the suon that spoke of pleasure and acceptance.

She heard no beckon but something reached out to her like the caress of a breeze and it drew her steps forward until she stood beside Lilley. He looked at her with some of the gold reflected in his eyes and she knew he wanted her to touch the king, so she did. She ran her palm along an outstretched foreleg and up across the broad white chest. The tightly paneled scales seemed pearlescent in the light, each of them perfect in their place. She felt the suon's massive heart pumping steady and strong against the wall of his chest. The small pulse of her own wrist seemed to echo it back. Lilley set his right hand beside hers, pale to her tan, and the diamondback ducked his chin and pushed his black muzzle against both their shoulders as they stood side by side.

i and family and i

She stroked the small scales between the golden eyes. They watched her with a calm recognition. "Will you name him?" she asked.

"He's got one already." Lilley looked at her. "Raka."

The suon allowed them to strap their gear to his back and seat themselves along the diamond pattern of his spine. Méka wrapped her arm around Lilley's chest as the king unfurled his wings and rose half-way onto his hindquarters to walk forward toward the edge of the cliff and the sheer drop to the sea. The sun was setting rapidly in the west, the color of flames licking the violet onset of the sky. The sky above with its countless stars like an iridescent beach on the shores of a deepening dusk. The moon a fat pale eye over their shoulders in watchful benevolence and the country ahead waiting liminal and foreign for the inevitable night.

ACKNOWLEDGMENTS

So MANY PEOPLE are responsible for shepherding a book to readers and I need to thank them all. My amazing agent Tamara Kawar at DeFiore & Company, for her enthusiastic support, professional acuity, and editorial insight. As the first reader after myself, she was elemental in helping me to hone these ideas into something more in keeping with the vision I had of Méka's story. Thank you to all the wonderful people at Solaris: my editor Amy Borsuk for loving the stories from the start, for her kind incisiveness and complete understanding of this world and its people. It makes an author feel seen and she is a joy to work with. Artist and designer Sam Gretton for the absolutely stunning covers that capture what I hope is the uniqueness of this world and its dragons. Copyeditor Charlotte Bond for catching all of my mistakes and challenging me on how I think of my writing, from the macro to the minutiae. All writers need that. Thank you to Jess Gofton and Natalie Charlesworth for the diligent work and guidance through the media and marketing commitments writers engage in. It's fun! And to all the other people on the team who I would love to meet one day so I can thank you in person.

Thank you to my family for being excited and supportive right along with me on this unpredictable journey of publishing. Thank you to steadfast friends who read my work but also share the love of creative expression: Winifred Wong, my day one who told me, "I want more of Greatmother's camp!" Derek Molata for all the many dinners and discussions about writing, life, and Formula 1. Thank you also for opening up the Tipsy Mermaid and providing a space for retreat, writing, and reflection. To the Sister Circle, incredible writers all: Noël Rivera, Stephanie Hill, Susanne Noorani, and Tara Burke, for sharing their worlds with me and giving a space to share in return. For checking in with one another too; all of us on the creative journey of writing and life need that sometimes.

Thank you to all my readers and fellow authors who have accompanied me on this journey at some point along the way, offering support and connection no matter the country in which we reside. Some things are truly borderless. Thank you to the bloggers, journalists, podcasters, bookstagrammers, and anyone who has ever signal boosted my work—it all matters. I've met so many great people through publishing and we all share one thing in common: a love of knowledge, storytelling, and reading. The world needs that more than ever.

ABOUT THE AUTHOR

KARIN WAS BORN in South America, grew up in Canada, and worked in the Arctic. She has been a creative writing instructor, adult education teacher, and volunteer in a maximum security prison. Her novels have been translated into French, Hebrew, and Japanese, and her short stories have been published in numerous anthologies, best-of collections, and magazines. When she isn't writing, she serves at the whim of a black cat.

FIND US ONLINE!

www.rebellionpublishing.com

/solarisbooks   /solarisbks   /solarisbooks

SIGN UP TO OUR NEWSLETTER!

rebellionpublishing.com/newsletter

YOUR REVIEWS MATTER!

Enjoy this book? Got something to say?

Leave a review on Amazon, GoodReads or with your
favourite bookseller and let the world know!